Boomer Boys

Stephen Davis

Gemini Books—Lizella, GA
ISBN: 978-0-578-81886-3
Library of Congress Control Number: 2020925107
Title: *Boomer Boys*
Author: Stephen Davis
Digital distribution | 2020
Paperback | 2020

Dedication

Dedicated to the memory of my father, Vernon L. Davis, the source of my inspiration for this book and for much of the material contained herein.

Prologue

The white frame farm house shimmered in the late afternoon heat, appearing from a distance to be a mirage in the center of an oasis of pecan trees. It sat back from the main road, a rough dirt track, which could be transformed from a dust bowl to a quagmire in minutes depending upon the severity of the rain. The trek from the road to the house was nearly a quarter mile, just the right distance to provide an entertaining stroll when it was time to fetch the mail as the old man who lived there often did. The rutted drive was lined on either side by dilapidated barbed wire fencing that hinted of having once been stretched tightly between wooden fence posts but now appeared hell bent on pulling those posts right out of the ground. The posts themselves were each uniquely grotesque with no two matching, the result of having been replaced or repaired at odd times over the years but rarely two at the same time. For the most part, they still performed their intended purpose of keeping the cows confined to their one hundred acre pasture, but it was not an uncommon occurrence to be called by one of the neighbors to "come git your blasted cows out of my garden!" Of course, it was just as likely that the neighbor's cows would be the ones creating havoc in *your* garden so no one really took these adventurous bovine forays too seriously.

The old house was balanced precariously upon a series of "pillars" which were nothing more than stacks of rocks supporting it on the corners with a few inner columns placed strategically to hold up the floor. A stone fireplace, merely a larger stack of rocks rising from ground level to a few feet above the roof line, dominated the side of the house where the living room was located. Not much grass grew in the yard which was in constant shade from the spreading limbs of the pecan trees. This would seem to be a good thing when weighed against the necessity of constantly mowing the lush lawns of some of the neighboring farms, but since Gramma insisted that the yards be swept clear of debris every day, it was a dubious advantage at best. The debris in question could be anything from dead frogs the kids had dragged up from the creek to chicken droppings generated by the flock constantly roaming the property.

Luther Skidmore, ("Gramps") was a fifth generation owner of this piece of dirt. He had inherited the farm from his daddy, Abner, who had inherited it from his daddy William, who had inherited it from his daddy, Joshua, who had inherited from his daddy, Caleb, who had inherited it from a local boy he had befriended during the Civil War. The lad had gotten himself killed at the Battle of Atlanta, but before going on to his reward, he had written a will, leaving the farm to Caleb who he claimed was his only friend. The boy had said he had no living relatives, the result of an outbreak of scarlet fever which had claimed his mother, father, brother and sister in quick succession, leaving him as the lone heir. Having no other direction in his life, he had joined the Confederate army and served well until his unfortunate encounter with one of General Sherman's skirmishers. He had once told Caleb, "Ain't nothing there for me to go back to an' I don't think Ah'm gone make it anyways, so I want you to see if you kin make a go of it. It's good land but I just cain't go back there where all I knew was heartache!" Caleb had tried to reassure his friend that his future was all in front of him but the boy knew better and would not be deterred from executing the will naming Caleb as his sole beneficiary. After the war, Caleb had returned to his native state of Texas, and tried a few odd jobs with little real success. He had practically forgotten the will stored in his old chest full of Civil War memorabilia. He dug it out one night and re-read its contents, deciding on the spot that he had nothing to lose by coming to Georgia and at least looking the place over. He made the trip by horseback, camping and living off the land and the good will of Confederate sympathizers along the way. He finally arrived in south Georgia and after making several inquiries, located the long-deserted farm. He was initially disappointed when he saw the weed-grown fields and dilapidated house, but despite the farm's woeful state of disrepair, he could see its potential. He presented the will to the local magistrate and, to his great surprise, no one contested it. The document was recorded and he soon became the owner of two hundred acres of prime bottomland within spitting distance of the Altamaha River. The run-down little, one-room house, after some minor repairs, was adequate for his needs and he moved in immediately. Having no other prospects, he decided that he would try his hand at farming. Having no resources to stake his venture, he sold his horse and acquired a mule, a bottom plow and a few seeds. With this meager beginning, he began his venture on a very small scale.

The fertile soil near the river proved to be excellent. Within a year, he was producing some fine crops, including corn, peanuts and potatoes. By means of bartering with his neighbors he had acquired a few head of livestock, providing the basis for a cow herd. He married in 1873 and soon begat his first born, Joshua. As the family grew, rooms were "added on" several times over the succeeding generations of Skidmores. A barn and a smokehouse along with several smaller outbuildings had been built as needs had arisen. Additional acreage was cleared and cultivated until the farm took its present shape. His methods had changed little in the past fifty years. Oh, there were minor changes attempted such as the time when Luther's son, Ernest had come home from college with some grandiose ideas about turning the farm into a showplace and he had made some improvements in the way farming was done, introducing tractors and some other mechanized contraptions but all in all, things remained pretty much the same.

Ernest had married his high school sweet heart, Eileen Smith and soon had produced two offspring, a boy which they named Rodney after one of Ernest's fraternity buddies and a girl they called Eleanor, or "Ellie" for short. Initially, Rod and Ellie were barely tolerated by their grandfather who had long ago determined "to have no truck with youngun's. All they do is want everything they see and worry you to death about it". He considered them, as well as the majority of their generation to be "spoiled brats." That attitude prevailed for almost three years. It was then that he heard Ellie bragging at her birthday party to one of her friends that "I bet my grandpa knows everything that your grandpa knows and then some. He's the best grandpa in the whole wide world." He had been lying back in his recliner scarcely aware of the party going on around him when these words reached his ears. Overcome with shame for his previous attitude, he suddenly felt an overwhelming urge to prove his granddaughter's point. His creaky old body suddenly felt thirty years younger. Rising from his seat, he hovered over Ellie like some giant from a fairy tale. " Now, Ellie," he began, " You don't know if I'm the best grandpa in the whole world, you haven't met 'em all have you?" As he scooped up her giggling, wiggly body, a transformation occurred which he could not account for. As much as she and Rod had aggravated him, he came to the realization in that moment that they would all too soon be out of their childhoods and want less and less to do with him as they got older and became more involved with their own lives. He recalled with painful regret how that very thing had occurred with his own son faster than he could have believed possible. He determined then and there to give them as much of himself as he was capable of giving in the time he had left with them. They had been inseparable ever since, spending time fishing, walking in the woods, tending the farm animals and just enjoying each other's company during the course of each day.

Now here they were, he in his hammock and they in their lawn chairs, all of them sipping on glasses of iced lemonade which "Gramma" Skidmore had just delivered before scurrying off to do some household chore or other. She rarely participated in the daytime activities of the threesome, citing that "A woman's work is never done!" Her time with the grandchildren was mostly in the evenings when she would read to them or play games before getting them ready for bed. Gramps had learned not to interfere with them during her time so she returned the favor by "letting them be" during their time. It was an arrangement which seemed to work just fine.

Like most June days in South Georgia, it was hot! The sun was like a giant radiant heater that you wished you could move just a few feet further from. The only relief was the shade provided by the spreading branches of the pecan tree and the rare hint of a breeze which brushed their faces and left them wishing for more. The animals had all disappeared, seeking whatever shade they could find. Two of the dogs were stretched out under the car and a couple more, the bigger ones, of course, had sought the prime spots underneath the house which were always cool and damp even on the hottest days.

The hammock was always reserved for Gramps. Several years ago, one of his old fishing buddies had given it to him at a birthday party as a gag gift, accompanied by a crude comment to the effect that, "Now your lazy carcass has some place to lie besides the sofa!" What his friend did not know was that Gramps' father had had a hammock just like this one and Gramps had dearly loved to lie in it whenever he got a chance which was not often. Far from taking offense, Gramps was grateful for the gift (although he never let on to his friend) and soon had it strung up between the trunk of a large pecan tree and a stout post he had set in the ground for just that purpose. He took to reclining in the hammock shortly after lunch on most days and spending a couple of hours just relaxing with his eyes closed. He never admitted to actually sleeping but sometimes Gramma was sure she heard noises resembling snores emanating from his direction.

Today Rod and Ellie were here for their annual visit from the city so he was trying his best to hold off the nap which was persistently nagging at him. They came to spend three or four weeks with their grandparents each summer. Unfortunately, at least in his eyes, they had been raised as "city kids" and were totally ignorant of the ways of the farm. But since beginning their annual summer visits a couple of years ago, they had spent enough time around the farm that they were no longer shocked by the "facts of life" which confronted them on a regular basis. The sights of dogs or cows or chickens in the act of mating were so commonplace that they scarcely even commented on it any more. When these visits had first begun, Gramps was less than enthusiastic about the intrusion upon his time, considering them to be nothing but "little nuisances, following me around all the time, asking dumb questions and constantly getting in my way," but they had eventually worked their charms and he always found himself dreading the time for their departure as it neared each year.

Gramps was not overly prone to emotional

demonstrations. Having lived through the post WWII years, and then been assailed by the turmoil surrounding the Vietnam War, he had developed a stoic acceptance of bad times as a necessary part of life to compare the good times to and spent little time contemplating his lot in life. He knew it could have been better but he also knew it could have been much worse. That had been abundantly demonstrated to him as his father told about many of their neighbors who had lost their farms during the tough economic years of the thirties. His own grandfather, William, had barely escaped with his holdings intact. The depression years had been tough on everyone. After taking over control of the farm, Gramps had been fortunate enough to guess right about the types of crops to plant over the years more often than not and consequently had made enough money to survive and hold off the creditors. He had certainly not gotten rich but he had developed a great sense of pride. Having finally made enough to pay off everyone he owed, he now considered himself independent. He could produce whatever he needed with his own labor on his own land and not be beholding to anyone. That was his personal measure of success. He had spent the better part of thirty years working his regular job on the railroad, but had always managed to keep at least some of his land under cultivation. One year it might be corn, the next year peas or peanuts. His genes demanded that he grow something, though, and it mattered little to him what particular crop he planted each year. He doubted that anyone would continue planting after he was gone, what with his son living comfortably as a lawyer in Atlanta and the grand kids constantly talking about being nurses, doctors or ball players. But as long as he was able, he vowed, he would see that something was planted each year. This year, he had planted watermelons and they were already as big as footballs and would soon be ready to harvest. His retirement and Social Security income was adequate for his needs, so he now planted only for the pure satisfaction of seeing something grow. He hoped that someday the kids would learn the joy of reaping the earth's bounty as much as he did now.

With this new-found sense of independence, he began to realize that there were more things in life which should be enjoyed than merely survival. The visits of the grandkids became eye opening experiences for him. He had always taken the miracles of nature for granted. The sight of a new-born calf had meant the herd was growing and that meant more money when they were sold. A tiny chicken emerging from inside an egg had previously meant only that there would be more chicken dinners this year. A butterfly was just there; he never considered the miracle which had preceded its arrival. Rod and Ellie had seen these events and many more as marvelous, miraculous happenings which needed explaining. Their questions filled his ears daily. He was dismayed to find that he often had no plausible explanation for many of their inquiries. Far from being discouraged, though, he determined that he would find the answers. After all, he couldn't have his grandchildren thinking he was an ignorant old man. Faint smiles which had been absent from his face for years, began to appear, crinkling the corners of his mouth at the most unexpected times. In the short span of one summer, he was transformed from the local curmudgeon to the embodiment of Santa Claus. To most of his acquaintances, he was still a cranky, crotchety old man, but to the kids he was the next best thing to candy apples. He was their Gramps and they would listen to nothing negative about him. So what if he was a little touchy at times. A person his age had certainly earned the right.

Rod and Ellie had come to look forward to their summer visits to the country almost as much as the old man did. As soon as the first faint signs of Spring arrived, they knew summer could not be far behind and began marking the calendar, counting down the days. Although other short visits were made during the year, summer was the big one and by far their favorite. Their forays into the woods and fields around Gramps' house were like small adventures to them. They always seemed to find something new to be amazed at. And he always seemed to be willing to share his time with them. And now they were ready for the best time of all: the time spent under the pecan tree, listening to Gramps tell the tales of his boyhood. How much of what he told was truth and how much was imagination expanded by fading memory, they did not know nor did they care. He certainly was not above embellishing the details a little to add some spice to a story, but that made it all the more enjoyable in their adoring minds. Today was the third day of their visit but the first opportunity they had had to be alone with Gramps. The first two days had been spent visiting the neighbors or having visits from the neighbors, the sole purpose of which was to get themselves "shown off". They had heard the phrase, "They've just shot up like weeds!" so often they began to fear someone would actually take a hoe to them and cut them back down to size. Gramps would strut around like a barnyard rooster during these visits while the women, in his words, "tried to wear out their lips on the young'uns." He was not very tolerant of hen parties and soon found an excuse for himself and the kids to take a stroll around whatever land they happened to be on. Their wanderings usually ended up at the nearest farm pond or creek. The old man just seemed to be drawn to water. Gramma said he was like a thirsty cow, the way he was always looking for a body of water. "He must have gills in there somewhere," she would exclaim, "'Cause if he don't get near some water ever' blessed day, he nearly chokes!" Even he had to admit to a serious affinity for bodies of water.

He had other "cravings" as well such as a taste for a good plug of *Red Man,* a nip of "rheumatism medicine" before bed and a hankering to sleep in the woods from time to time. "It just ain't natural to have a roof blocking out the stars every night," he would say. Gramma had long since accepted these afflictions and tolerated them as part of his nature, even if not fully giving her approval. They had made an unspoken pact early in their marriage that they had fallen in love with each other just as they were and there was no good reason to try to change someone you loved.

Gramps had taken to telling the kids story after story about his childhood. He said he was one of the first in the generation following World War II which were now being called "Baby Boomers".

During the days of his boyhood, he had thought that his family had little to be proud of. They were never deprived of food or clothing, it was true, but neither had they been of the privileged class. They wore "hand-me-down" clothes and camped out on their vacations. They had never spent even one night in a motel. Gramps and his friends spent most of their boyhood days without adult supervision, often leaving the house shortly after sunrise and not returning until dark. They entertained themselves by fishing, hunting, "walking the creek" or playing pickup games of baseball or football. They loved nothing better than camping out overnight in the woods with no adults present. Gramps marveled now at the leniency of his parents in allowing such activities. Nowadays, everything had to be organized! You never saw a group of kids playing a pickup baseball game or just walking around in the woods looking for adventure. To be sure, today's kids have plenty of activities, but they are all planned in advance and supervised and so *structured.* What a difference a couple of generations have made. Well, he intended to show these kids that there were many ways to enjoy life without so much structure. He had discovered that the best way for him to do this was to tell them of his own experiences. He did this on a regular basis and he and the kids had come to look forward to his tales and stories as the high points in their days. In between the telling of the tales, he had tried to demonstrate to them what it had been like by inviting them to walk with him back in time to experience things unique to his generation. Since he had only the male perspective, he called his collection of characters: *Boomer Boys.* What follows is a collection of stories as told by Gramps Skidmore. Any resemblance of the characters in these stories to real people is entirely intentional. Of course, where memory has faded, embellishment has been added. Please excuse where necessary. Thank you for your indulgence.

Chapter 1
The Hazards of Hammocks

That familiar, far-away look came into the old man's eyes and the kids knew he was about to launch into a tale. As the recipients of many of Gramps' stories in the past, they had come to not only indulge the old man, but to actually cherish the times he was willing to share his former life with them. The stories were not only entertaining, they also provided glimpses into a part of their family history with which they would otherwise have had no inkling. They had never been disappointed and did not expect to be now.

He began as he usually did by asking, "Did I ever tell you about the time …" It was a signal as subtle as a Roman Candle. Their attention to him was immediate and complete as he continued, "… my friend, Pork was attacked by a hammock? Worst accident I ever seen where no one actually got killed. But I don't guess ya'll care to be bored by the ramblings of an old codger like me, do you?"

"But we want to hear about it, Gramps," Ellie squealed.

"Yeah, Gramps," Rod piped up, "You can't lead us on like that and then <u>not</u> tell us the story. That sure ain't fair."

"<u>Is'nt</u> fair Rod. <u>Is'nt</u> fair. You kids need to learn proper English! Now where was I?"

The intensity of their eyes as they focused on his face was all the encouragement he needed. They were not about to deny their Grandpa one of his chief pleasures in life. Encouraged by their expectant gazes, he began:

"Well, it was a hot summer day a lot like today. My friend, Pork had just got him a new 'bait caster' rod and reel which he considered his prize possession and was real eager to try it out. I'll tell you the story of the 'bait caster' later but right now all you need to know is that it was a fishin' pole."

"Pork had called an hour earlier and said he'd been excused from his daily chores since his father was taking a load of hogs to market and wouldn't be needin' him anymore that day. Sometimes when he went into town, Pork's dad made a short stop into Buddy's, the local tavern, a place where Pork was not allowed. That was fine with him since he sure didn't want to waste a rare afternoon off sittin' around listenin' to a bunch of old geezers swap tales."

"Pork had mounted his bicycle and begun the eight mile trek to our house. Me and my best friend, Weed decided to wait for him in the shade of the very pecan tree we're sittin' under now. My Dad had a hammock in those days strung up in the exact same place this one is now. Lucky for me, on that day Weed beat me to the hammock and was soon stretched out full length in it, enjoyin' the cool breeze. I grabbed a seat in a handy lawn chair nearby, giving me a ring side seat to one of the most spectacular events I have ever witnessed. An' believe me, I've seen some doozies. 'Course at that time I had no idea what was 'bout to happen and felt pretty miffed at relinquishing the hammock."

"For a 12-year old boy forty pounds overweight, Pork could move pretty good but it would still take him close to an hour to make the ride. His bicycle, 'Old Faithful' bears some comment. To fully grasp the mental image of the events to follow, you need to know something about this bike. It was a piece-meal affair whose parts had been scavenged from various back yards and junk piles over the past three or four years or in trades for knives, marbles or baseball cards. The front wheel was considerably smaller than the rear, causing the rider to be crouched in a perpetual 'racin' posture', rear end in the air and head down to the level of the handle bars. It was without fenders too, those having been discarded as being too much trouble to keep re-attaching each time they fell off or had to be removed while patching tires."

"The composite vehicle resembled some Rube Goldberg contraption whose parts worked in a mysterious, unexplainable sequence of events which had to occur in exactly in the correct order to effect the desired forward motion. Although there was a chain guard, a necessity to keep his pants legs from getting wrapped in the chain, it was hanging on by only one loose screw, causing it to set up a horrific scraping racket at each turn of the sprocket. Pork had no need to announce his arrival anywhere he went on this machine as anyone not completely deaf could hear him coming a mile away."

"A small wooden basket, formerly used for holding peaches, was wired to the handle bars and carried Pork's prize possessions, three bass lures, each of which resembled a large colorful cigar adorned with grappling hooks. Also present was a small square metal box which only a few minutes before had held the household supply of Band Aids. It now contained a few assorted hooks, a couple of plastic bobbers and a handful of 'split shot' which rattled as he rolled, which just added to the racket produced by the chain guard."

"Slung across the handle bars was the previously mentioned 'bait caster'."

"He was now huffing and puffing up the last long hill outside town. Sweat drenched his body, but caused him no concern, his only thoughts being those of catching some of those 'titty bream' Calvin Tucker had told him about. Calvin was the proprietor of the Super Glow Service Station and had introduced Pork to this term in describing a mess of bream he'd caught to Pork's father, Jack. He had professed that they had caught no fewer than fifty last week and had exclaimed, "Jack, no lie at least half of 'em was 'titty bream'. Pork's head had snapped around at the mention of fishin' although he was perplexed at his lack of knowledge of this terminology. He'd been fishin' all his life and had yet to see a fish exhibiting this particular anatomical feature. 'That surely can't be true', he had thought, 'But who knows, maybe if they get big enough …'

"Curiosity finally getting the better of him, he just had to ask. 'Mr. Calvin,' he began, 'Just how big does a fish have to get before it grows titties?' Both Calvin and Mr. Campbell's bellies shook as they attempted to suppress their amusement. Pork just sat silently, wondering what the joke was. 'Now, son,' Calvin smiled, 'The fish don't grow no titties.'"

"'Well why …'" Pork began.

"'Because that's what you call 'em when they's so big you cain't get your hand around 'em and you gotta hold 'em against your chest to git the hook out! That's why you call 'em titty bream. Lord A'mighty, fish with breasts! Not a bad notion though, huh, Jack?'"

"Jack, now red-faced himself, allowed as how it was getting' late and they had to go as he hurried out the door before Pork asked any more embarrassin' questions."

So engrossed was he in the telling of his story, Gramps had forgotten the ages of his audience. Some snickering and giggling from their direction abruptly reminded him. He realized that a change of subject was in order.

"You kids ready for some more lemonade?" he asked. They each filled their glasses with the iced beverage and settled back for the rest of the story. The groundwork now having been laid, they knew he was about to get to the best part.

Gramps resumed: "Well, me and Weed heard Pork coming long we saw him, what with that chain guard scraping loud as a chain saw. As he topped the hill and began the steep descent preceding the entrance to the yard, there was a conspicuous change in sounds. We knew something was wrong. The regular rhythm of 'scraaaaape! …scraaaaape!... scraaaaape!…' had suddenly been replaced by a series of staccato yelps emanating from Pork: 'LOOK OUT!... CHAIN'S OFF!...CLEAR THE WAY!!!...YA'LL LOOK OUT!'

"Soon enough, Pork's bulk could be seen through the trees astraddle his bike which was fish-tailing wildly. It was clear that Pork had little control since without a chain, he had no brakes. As the dust cloud grew closer, we became concerned for Pork's well being. We should have worried more about our own."

"As Pork careened into the yard, he side-swiped the beat-up old pickup parked there, narrowly missing a head-on collision. Underneath the truck, soundly sleeping was Weed's collie dog, Rory, whose only appendage extending outside the truck's body, was his tail on which Pork's tires made a direct hit."

"Rory, forgetting that he was under the truck, shot to his feet, or I should say, he would have, had his head not whacked the low hangin' muffler. Now he was hurting at both ends and he meant to have some revenge. Spying Pork rattling by just a few yards away, he quickly decided upon his victim."

"Now Rory had some history with Pork, involving an oscillating fan and Rory's tail which had occurred a few months back. The memory of that painful experience was forever imprinted on his feeble mind. His hatred of Pork had grown every day since."

"And now here he was again, adding more misery to Rory's life. He shot out from under the car, and in two long leaps, caught up with Pork, grabbing his pants leg in his teeth and snapping his head backward while jamming his legs into the ground, resulting in a rapid halt to the bike's momentum. Pork's foot was ripped from the pedal, causing an abrupt downward motion of his entire body."

"The first object of resistance encountered was the cross bar, which made solid contact with Pork's crotch. For an instant, Pork could see nothing but blinding stars and was aware of nothing but the excruciating, white-hot pain between his legs. Letting go of the handlebars, he grabbed the crossbar with both hands in an effort to prevent further damage to his body but, at the same time, eliminating his ability to steer."

"Weed looked up from his precarious perch on the hammock just in time to see Pork, Old Faithful and Rory bearing down on him at break-neck speed. With no time to properly dismount, Weed's only avenue of escape was to flip the hammock over, spilling his lanky frame to the ground with a jolt. Pork opened his eyes just in time to see Weed's hasty exit, but not in time to employ any evasive action himself."

"Boy, bike and dog sailed into the hammock in a tangle of elbows, knees, hair, fishhooks and metal, straining its fabric to the limit as it swung into the air. It then rebounded, swung back in the opposite direction and began spinning, entrapping Pork, Rory and the bike inside."

"After several flips, the hammock came to rest. Like a huge cocoon giving birth to some alien creature, the hammock began to wiggle and squirm with a leg poking out here, a handlebar there, a hairy foot there. The cocoon's occupants were immobilized except for Rory's teeth, which had shifted from Pork's pants to his ankle and were now clamped firmly in place as his head began a vigorous shaking motion accompanied by the most vicious snarling Pork had ever heard. Several of the hooks from Pork's monster bass lures were imbedded in various locations on his body."

"By this time, the level of pain in Pork's crotch had subsided a few degrees and he became aware of a new source of discomfort, this one coming from the area of his left ankle. He was still unaware of exactly what had caused this calamity and could not maneuver his head into a position to see his feet. Desperately seeking some relief, he screamed, 'Weed, somethin's eatin' my ankle. Can you quit laughin' long enough to untangle this mess? "

"Weed was gripped in a paroxysm of uncontrollable laughter by this time and could not have helped if he'd wanted to. And he was enjoyin' the scene way too much to want to. His initial giggles had now given way to full-fledged guffaws as he rolled around on the ground below the wiggling cocoon. Finally, he gained enough control to drag himself to his feet."

"He could hardly decide where to begin his efforts to free the cocoon's occupants. Rory was still growling and gnawing Pork's ankle, Pork was still screaming for help and a few parts of the bike were visible, sticking out at various angles from the hammock. The needle-sharp hooks only added to Pork's misery. Weed knew he had to take action soon or some real damage could occur."

"His first words were not what Pork wanted to here; 'Don't worry Rory, old man. I'll get you out of there,' he began."

"'Weed, you miserable excuse for a friend, how about taking care of me before you worry about your stupid mutt,' Pork screamed."

"'Oh well, if you prefer, I'll just let him keep gnawing on your ankle.'"

"'OK,' he said, "Do what you gotta do, but just get him off me'"

"A few minutes later, Weed finally untangled the last of the rope supporting the writhing mass and Pork flopped to the ground, making a sound sorta' like a full water bottle dropped on the floor."

"'Oomph,' he grunted, 'Shoulda stayed home and cut corn. At least there, there ain't no rabid hounds around.'"

"Weed displayed the same amount of sympathy he usually did when observing the misfortune of others, which is none. 'Pork,' he began, 'This ain't nearly as bad as your bike wreck on Breezy Hill.'"

"'Shut up, Weed!' was Pork's response to that. 'How would you know? All you did was laugh then, too!'"

"'Yeah, you're right, I just can't help it,' Weed admitted. 'You just keep doing such dumb things!'"

"Over the last few years, Pork's penchant for disaster had become legendary. He seemed to have several major incidents every year, not to mention the numerous 'minor' ones often experienced in attempting the most routine of tasks. Grace was not a word often used in the same sentence with his name."

"What he did have in abundance, though, was persistence. Once he set his mind to a task, there was little that would stop him. The encounter with the hammock was no different. He had left home intending to go fishing and he was not about to be deterred by such a minor mishap. He dragged himself up from the ground and began to gather his equipment as though he had just made a routine dismount. His fishing rod was intact, having been thrown clear and his scattered tackle was quickly gathered. Luckily most of the hooks were not imbedded past the barbs and were easily backed out, leaving a series of red puncture wounds on his arms and legs, each dribbling a tiny blood trail."

"Weed couldn't believe what he was seeing. 'Just what do you think you're doing', he asked."

"' Why, what do you think? I'm going fishin', was Pork's quick response."

"'Man, you've probably got broken bones, not to mention rabies. You need to go to the emergency room,' Weed advised."

"'No way. I don't get many days off and I sure ain't gonna spend it in the hospital,' he insisted."

"Weed could see that Pork's mind was set. He tried a new approach. 'Well, let me at least call your momma.'"

"'Naw, man. She'd want me to come home for sure. I'm Ok, I tell you.'"

"'Are you sure?' Weed was skeptical.

"'Sure I'm sure,' Pork snapped. 'Now if you want to go, get your stuff and let's get goin'. If I need to go to the hospital, I can always go tomorrow. Today, I'm gonna fish.'"

"'You're hopeless,' Weed relented. 'Come on. Let's get some bait.'"

Chapter 2
The Bait Caster

Gramps sat on the edge of the hammock and waited for the kids to join him. Rod and Ellie were a little late getting out of bed this morning. It was the second day of their annual summer visit to Gramps' and Gramma's house and they always seemed to sleep a little better out in the country, with windows open, fresh air drifting in on the breeze. Gramma had had to make several calls to rouse them, but she finally convinced them to get moving because Gramps was going to the pond later and he was not going to wait on them. After a hurried breakfast of grits, eggs and bacon, they were ready and anxious to face the day. Finishing the meal off, they sprinted from the table, intending to join Gramps where they knew he would be: under the shade of the pecan tree.

"Not so fast, you two!" Gramma called. "Ya'll have got a coupla' things to do before wastin' the rest of your day listenin' to the ramblin's of an old man."

"Aw, Gramma," Rod whined. "We want to get going. Daylights wasting" It was a term Gramps often used when he was in a hurry and Rod figured Gramma had heard it before. He was right, she had, but it had no more effect on her when Rod said it then it did coming from Gramps.

"Now, I don't know what ya'll do at your Daddy's

house but here, we brush our teeth and make our bed *before* leavin' the house," Gramma stated.

"Yes, ma'am but Gramps said he wanted to get an early start," Ellie chimed in.

"True, but he'll just have to hold his horses a few more minutes. Cleanliness is next to Godliness, you know." Gramma was insistent.

They both knew there was no need to argue, so they climbed back up the stairs and took care of the chores, bounding back down in record time.

"I better not find those beds messed up," Gramma warned as they flew past.

"You, won't, Gramma," they promised, hitting the screen door on the run and letting it slam behind them.

The old lady just shook her head, amazed at the instantaneous transformation which had just occurred, namely that of changing the kids from zombies to world class sprinters in the space of a few short minutes. Even so, she resumed her cleaning with just the hint of a smile on her face.

The kids found Gramps just as they had expected to, sitting on the hammock, whittling on a small stick as he whistled softly to himself.

"What you making, Gramps?" Ellie asked.

"Oh nothing," he assured her. "Just whittlin'"

"Why?" Rod wanted to know.

"Oh, no particular reason," Gramps responded. "It's just somethin' I do to relax."

"Seems like a waste of time," Ellie snorted.

"Well, not everything you do has to produce something, young lady. Some things you do just for the sheer pleasure of it. Whittlins' one of 'em," Gramps said.

"Can I try it?" Rod asked.

"We'll have to see about getting' you a knife, young man. Just as soon as you convince me you can handle it safely," Gramps promised.

"Great! When will that be?" Rod wanted to know.

"All in due time, son. All in due time." Gramps was fond of making vague promises, knowing that, without a specific time frame, he could not be pinned down. They would just have to live with it.

"Hey, before I forget," Gramps adeptly changed the subject. "You kids remember me promisin' to tell you the story of Old Pork's 'bait caster'?"

"Yessir, we sure do. It was just yesterday, Gramps!" Ellie reminded him.

"Oh, so it was," Gramps admitted. "So what am I waitin' for?"

"Nothing, Gramps." Rod assured him. "We're ready to hear about it now."

"Well, I guess we've got time. Charley said he'd meet us at his pond in about an hour. That's enough time for this tale."

"First off, do either of you know what a 'bait caster is?" he asked.

"Nossir, we don't, except that we figured it must be some kind of fishing pole," Rod said.

"Right you are. But not just any kind of fishin' pole." The old man stated. "It's a special kind that not many ever learn to use properly. Another name for it is a 'level wind' meaning that the line, usually a heavy braided line, is wound on a horizontal spool which is attached to the rod near the butt. The difficulty in casting with this reel is that the line comes off the spool only as fast as the spool itself can spin. Sometimes, the rate of spin of the spool does not exactly match the speed of the line coming off and a terrible tangle of line called a 'backlash' or 'bird's nest' is produced. Some form of profanity usually follows this event."

"Gosh, Gramps, if it's so hard, why did people even use them," Rod wanted to know.

"'Cause there weren't nothin' else," Gramps huffed. "We sure didn't like 'em, but we had no choice but to use 'em or be limited to the length of a cane pole for castin'. 'Course the bait casters of today with their ball bearings and braking systems are much easier to use than the early models and almost all serious bassers use 'em. But believe me, it was a glorious day when spinnin' reels got invented! But let's get on with Pork's bait caster, OK?"

"Sure Gramps," they chimed in together.

"All right, then. Here it is."

"Pork had reason to be proud of his bait caster. He had seen it in the window of Mr. Pettigrew's hardware store almost a year before and knew he simply had to have it. He had just enough money to put it on layaway and then, to get the rest of the money, he took a paper route. It had taken him six months of getting up at dawn, sorting and banding newspapers and then pedaling the treacherous, ten mile route assigned to him. Along its length were located a series of houses whose owners must have thought their property needed some extraordinary protection since each of them owned wolf-like creatures, whose life's ambition appeared to be that of dragging Pork from his bicycle and ripping him into tiny pieces."

"After several shredded pairs of jeans and some minor bites on his ankles, Pork hit upon the idea of wearing a pair of rubber boots used by his dad while slogging around in the hog pens. Although their fragrance could be compared to the "honey pots" in most of the houses at the time, they served their purpose well and the dogs soon lost interest when Pork began slowing down and letting them chew on his ankles for fun.

"What's a 'honey pot', Gramps?" Ellie interjected.

"Oh yeah. I forgot how young ya'll are. Well, you might not believe it, but most folks didn't have indoor bathrooms until a few years ago and kept a jar in the bedroom to keep from having to make midnight trips to the privy"

"What's a privy?" It was Rod's turn to require an explanation for such a foreign term.

"Rod, you see that little square building down near the edge of the woods? That's a privy."

"But what's it for?" Rod was persistent.

"It's where we went to the bathroom," Gramps explained. "We had to walk down there whenever we had to go."

"You gotta' be kidding!" Rod gave Gramps an unbelieving look. He was used to Gramps pulling his leg on occasion and thought for sure this was one of those times.

"Nope. This time, I'm tellin' ya'll the truth. Believe me, it wasn't a very pleasant experience either."

Turning up their noses in disgust, Rod & Ellie both emitted loud statements of "EWWWW, gross!"

"Well, it's true. But the smell was only a minor annoyance. The big issue was dealing with spiders the size of small birds as well as wasps and scorpions which seemed to always sting you in the most inconvenient spots. You see, like I've been telling you, you don't realize how good you've got it. But anyway, let's get back to the story."

"In addition to the boots, Pork had another defensive

weapon. He carried a small squirt bottle of ammonia which he used when the creatures became a little too aggressive in their assaults."

"After a seemingly interminable period of this torture, the day finally arrived when he had enough money. He wasted no time in resigning his position as 'paper boy' in spite of the fierce protests from his boss who, no doubt wondered where he would find anyone else fool enough to carry that route."

"The first Saturday thereafter found Pork parked on the doorstep of Mr. Pettigrew's hardware store, his money clenched tightly in his hand, a good thirty minutes before opening time. By and by, he spied the ambling figure of Mr. Pettigrew, slowly making his way toward the store. Pork yelled, 'It's about time,' as the proprietor got within shoutin' distance. Pork was intent on demanding his prize."

"'Now, who have we here at such an early hour?' Mr. Pettigrew pretended ignorance of Pork's mission although he was well aware of who he was and what he was there for. He began fumbling with a huge ring of keys, as though befuddled as to which key might open the lock. 'Course he'd only been running that store for close to thirty-five years. With the trial of first one key then another, Pork's agitation grew. 'Come on, Mr. Pettigrew', he pleaded. 'Just let me try it. I'll get that door open!'"

"'Just hold your horses, big boy. I know that key's on here somewhere. Leastways, it was last night when I let my granddaughter play with it. Sure hope she didn't lose it!' He was really getting into his act, now. Pork began to get a real uneasy feeling, thinking the key was lost forever. Mr. Pettigrew took no notice of Pork's anxious looks. He just kept poking key after key at the uncooperative lock, whistling all the while like he hadn't a care in the world."

"Finally, he announced, 'Well, this one better be it. It's the last one!'"

"'Well hurry up an' try it. I ain't got all day, you know.' Ole Pork was gettin' desperate."

"'Let's just see'. Mr. Pettigrew mustered as much of a doubtful expression as he could, milking the situation to the max. He just couldn't resist making Pork suffer for at least a few more seconds. With a great show of effort, the proprietor put his shoulder to the door and shoved it open. Pork was by him in a flash, almost knocking the old man over in his haste. He had snatched the rod off the shelf, got it to the counter and produced his wad of bills before Mr. Pettigrew even got inside the store."

"'There it is, twelve dollars,' Pork shouted. 'Now let me get going so I can try this baby out!' He was beside himself with excitement, but Mr. Pettigrew wasn't through with him just yet."

"'Not so fast, young man,' he said as he ducked a side-arm whip cast which almost clipped his nose. Pork then froze in mid-cast as the next words from Mr. Pettigrew reached his ears. 'There's been a slight change in the price since last March.' Pork's stomach got all queasy as the message sank in. For a minute he thought he might actually throw up. He had never considered the possibility that the price might go up."

"The thought of having to return to the paper route caused his whole body to quiver. The memories of all those early morning wakeups, the tedium of sorting and banding papers, the hours of monotonous pedaling, the pain of numerous dog bites, all came flooding back into his mind as the possibility of that unhappy prospect became real. The change in his countenance must have been so profound and pitiful that Mr. Pettigrew could play with his emotions no longer."

"'Actually, son,' he announced with a twinkle in his eye, 'The price has come down. It's now only ten dollars. Plus tax, of course.'"

"Pork's face was immediately transformed from misery to ecstasy. He was speechless. He just stood there grinning, unable to find the proper words to express his gratitude. Mr. Pettigrew finally asked him if he was OK. Pork found his voice, assuring Mr. Pettigrew that he couldn't be better. He'd just realized that, not only could he buy the fishing rod, he would also have enough left over for some tackle. He quickly completed his shopping, picking out several of the largest lures he could find. His reasoning was that it would take a sure 'nough big 'un to attack any of those lures and he wasn't after no babies. And if ole Big Mama did get near his bait, he wanted to be sure at least one of those hooks was in the right place to find some fish flesh. His theory was: 'The more hooks, the better.'"

"The sale was soon completed and the magic words, 'It's all yours, son' were uttered along with some off hand comment about 'leaving some for the rest of us' which Pork did not hear, having already exited the building. He was still hugging his treasure as he pedaled out of sight, the grating of the chain guard announcing his departure."

"Now, kids, to call this bait caster a 'treasure' is sorta like calling a headache one of life's most pleasant experiences. On his best day, the devil himself couldn't have invented a crueler torture device. As I said, this was long before the smooth castin' spinning rods of today.

And it was long before bait casters were equipped with fancy brakin' systems and anti- backlash mechanisms they now have. Pork had determined that he would learn to use the thing or die tryin'."

"Every evening after supper he would grab the rod and head for the back yard to practice. The yard animals soon recognized these sessions as a time for getting out of range or at least well hidden. Up until now, he had only had access to his father's cane poles and knew nothing of the intricacies and finesse required in the operation of the average bait caster. It was a major step in his learning process the day Weed told him about 'thumbing'. Until then, he had assumed you were supposed to create a back lash on every cast and that it was normal procedure to spend the next few minutes unraveling the 'birds nest'."

"Of course, this enlightenment didn't completely eliminate back lashes; it just reduced their number and severity. Even so, progress was slow and he still got at least a small back lash almost every cast. But he was undaunted by such minor inconveniences. After a few hours of more or less random casts, he began to feel confident enough to try to hit something specific."

"His first target of opportunity was his mother's five gallon foot tub which he 'borrowed' and placed underneath the chinaberry tree. He attached a one-ounce lead weight and began zingin' bullets all over the yard. His first victim was his father's coon hound, Old Red. The only times Red ever showed much excitement was at suppertime and on the rare occasions he was taken coon huntin'. As usual, he was catching a nap in the shade when the misplaced missile caught him square in the rump."

"He must have been dreamin' of a big chase 'cause he

shot straight up into the air, his feet flying before they touched the ground. He scratched out of the yard, slingin' dirt and howlin' at the top of his lungs at every stride. Pork could only chuckle as he watched the terrified hound lumber out of sight. He hoped Old Red had sense enough to come back soon or his dad would require some 'explaining.' In a few minutes, the embarrassed hound came slinkin' back into the yard, wearing a sheepish look on his wrinkled face. "

"Lest he be caught unawares again though, he gave Pork a wide berth and crawled underneath the house, a sanctuary already populated by several other of the family dogs mixed in with a couple of cats."

"What Pork lacked in skill, he made up for in persistence, spurred on by the fact that he had plowed ten hard-earned dollars into this outfit and he was 'by God going to learn to use it!' He didn't think he could bear the humiliation he was sure to suffer at the hands of his friends who would no doubt question his manhood, not to mention his sanity if he failed to master such a simple device."

"His attitude shifted constantly from one of pride at making a particularly accurate cast to disgust as he once again sat down and began peeling line off the reel. At those time, he would have been happy to give the contraption to the first passerby he saw. Then the memories of all the hours spent earning the money would be dredged up and relived in his mind and he realized that all that effort would be wasted if he gave up."

"His successes, even though still rare, became slightly more commonplace. Ever so gradually, he began to get the 'feel' of it. That's the way it is with bait casters. They're much like fly rods in that regard. They look simple but are anything but. You just keep at it and eventually the 'feel' begins to grow. After a few more days, Pork could hit the spot every third or fourth cast. The 'spot' was now the space previously occupied by the tub."

"On his first bullseye, and resultant 'CLANG", his mother had flown out the door, demanding to know, 'What the heck was that racket?'. Discovering her tub sporting a fresh dent, she immediately rescued it from further damage, warning Pork that his fishin' pole looked about the right size to give him a good switchin' if he so much as looked at her tub again. 'Aw Mom, what am I supposed to use for a target now?' he whined."

"'I don't know and don't care so long as it ain't my tub!' she screamed. Pork knew when she had reached her limit so he wisely said no more."

"His new target became an old card board box whose 'thunk' was not nearly as satisfying as the loud 'clang' produced by the tub, but it would just have to do. It soon became a tattered pile of shredded paper as cast after cast whacked into it. Although it could hardly be said that he had mastered the finesse part of the exercise, he was gaining on the accuracy part."

"After several days, he finally felt confident that he could at least get his lure into the water without permanently disfiguring anyone. He was now ready to go fishin'. He used that old 'bait caster' for many years. I can't say he ever got good at it, but he did manage to catch a couple of trophy size bass before he was done."

"Well, kids. It's about time to load up the truck and go meet Charley. Ya'll ready?"

"You bet, Gramps," they chorused.

"You don't happen to still have a 'bait caster' do you?"

Rod inquired. “I’d kinda’ like to try one sometime”

“Not on your life, son. I got way too smart to fool with them things a long time ago! You couldn’t pay me to use one now,” Gramps stated emphatically. “If you want to try one, you’ll have to do that on your own. I wouldn’t advise it, though.”

“Oh well, I was just wondering,” Rod mused as he began walking toward the shed to gather their fishing equipment.

Chapter 3
The Great Wasp Wars

The little Carolina cork began to quiver as the eight year old girl watched it intently.

"Get ready, Ellie. He's got it. Now pick up your pole real easy when he starts to move off," Gramps instructed.

He could have saved his breath. Ellie had caught hundreds of bluegills in her young life and already had eleven in the cooler today. Gramps could never resist lending his expertise, though and she always indulged the old man. It was the least she could do, considering the time he was willing to devote to her and Rod. The cork began a slow movement to the left and suddenly disappeared with barely a ripple.

"Now, Ellie, now! Pull him up. Easy now." Gramps was much more excited than the girl was. Ellie had already started to raise the cane pole when the cork first began its dance. The hook went home with a solid connection and the tip of her pole dipped sharply. The line began making little circles in the water as the fish made its futile escape attempt. Applying steady pressure, Ellie soon brought the scrappy bluegill to the surface and slid him across the water to Gramps' waiting hands. The fish took his place next to the others in the cooler.

"That's an even dozen. Guess that'll be enough for supper tonight. Let's head on in," Gramps suggested as he began raising the anchor.

"Aw, Gramps, can't we catch a few more?" Ellie pleaded.

"It is temptin' since they're bitin' real good today. But a good sportsman, er, sports person should never take more than they can use. If we was to be greedy, and everyone else did the same, there'd soon be none for any of us." Gramps was always careful to illustrate the reasons behind the rules. That way, he figured they'd be less likely to break them.

Ellie knew he was right, of course. She had heard it all before. She reluctantly agreed that it was time to return home. Gramps raised the anchor and she deftly steered the 'john boat' the short distance to shore. As they beached the small boat, Rod came running towards them. He had been unable to join them today because of Little League practice and he could hardly wait to inspect their catch.

"Gramps! Ellie! Did ya'll catch any? Let me see 'em," he shouted as he ran.

"Just hold on son, you can see 'em all you want when you help clean 'em," Gramps warned.

"They're some real nice ones, Ellie. How many did you catch?", he asked.

"All of them," she said, "But I could never have done it without Gramps' help." The old man glowed at this. Ellie was already learning about the male ego.

Rod was envious. He and his sister had cultivated a fierce rivalry which became more evident with every life experience they shared. "Gramps," he pleaded, "Can't we go back for just a little while so I can catch a few?"

"Not today, son," Gramps replied. "But I'll make you a deal. If you can get up at dawn tomorrow, we'll see if you can match Ellie, OK?"

"You bet," Rod whooped. "I'll tell Gramma to set the clock. I'll be ready," he shouted as he tore off up the hill toward the house.

An hour later, the cleaned fish were in a dish pan, awaiting the expert preparations Gramma would minister before putting them in the frying pan. Her "secret ingredient" always produced the best fried fish they'd ever tasted. She said it was only an extra helping of love, but everyone suspected it was really was some secret ingredient. She never would tell, though so they had the good sense to leave it alone.

As was his custom after an early morning fishing trip, Gramps retired to his trusty old hammock hanging under the pecan tree to enjoy a cold glass of iced tea. Rod and Ellie soon joined him, taking their seats on padded wooden lawn chairs, iced glasses of lemonade in their hands.

"Gramps, that was the best bait we've ever used. What was it? Where'd you get it?" Ellie was very curious about new things and Gramps had been unwilling to talk much while they fished. "Scares the fish," he had said.

But now that that concern was past, he was willing to divulge his secret. "Oh, it ain't the easiest bait to gather, but there's nothing much better for bream when you can get 'em. You see, most animals are not too eager to have humans take their young away and wasps are no different. That's what we were using. Wasp larvae. Unborn wasps. I finally found a fool proof way to gather them, but before that, a coupla' my friends had an interesting experience trying to gather a few."

The kids' ears perked up as they could sense a story was on the way.

Gramps did not disappoint as he continued, "As usual, Pork and Weed were planning a fishing trip but also, as usual, had no bait and no money. Pork, who was always on the lookout for new fishing methods, said he had heard from his daddy's cousin's uncle that there was no better bait than wasp larvae and he knew where there was a huge nest."

"Weed was skeptical, stating 'Well, I never heard of such and besides, I doubt those wasps are going to give up their babies without a fight.'"

"'No, they're not,' Pork agreed, 'but I think we ought to be able to figure out how to get 'em. Surely, we're smarter than a bunch of insects, ain't we? Let's go see what we've got.'"

"Pork stood gazing up at the huge wasp nest which Weed had pointed out under the eave of his house. 'Good God', he said. 'There must be a thousand of them.'"

"'Yeah, there's enough larvae in that nest to last a week', Weed agreed"

"'But just how the heck are we supposed to get 'em? I don't think they're fixin' to give 'em up easy!. Why don't we just fish with lures today? I got some new ones I wanta try anyway?' Pork didn't like the looks of this one bit."

"'Well, I been studyin' the problem and I think I got it figured out,' Weed was trying to be reassuring. 'You see, I got my momma's broom and it'll just about reach the nest if you hold it on the end and jump a little.'"

"Alarm bells began ringing in Pork's head. 'What do you mean, me. It's your idea, you do it,' he began his argument. 'Besides, you're taller and faster than me. What's the matter? You scared?'"

"Weed quickly rebutted this accusation. 'Pork, who's

the fastest sprinter on the track team?' he asked"

"'You are,' admitted Pork".

"'Right, and who's the best high jumper?

"'You are, ' Pork again had to admit"

"'Right again. So I figure it's only logical for me to take on this mission.'"

"Pork didn't offer any resistance to this idea, Weed's arguments making a lot of sense to him."

"While he was not always the most prudent in his decisions, no one could accuse Weed of cowardice. He had logged more hours in detention and gotten more licks from Mr. Brown's paddle than anyone else in seventh grade. He loved nothing better than showing off and this was just another great opportunity to build his reputation. He was already imagining the admiration coming his way if he pulled this off. 'OK, you big sissy, I'll show you how it's done. What I'm gonna do is run by and slap the nest down with the broom. Then, as soon as the wasps clear out, we can pick it up and go fishin'. And if that don't work, we'll go to Plan B, OK?'"

"'Uh, right, Weed,' Pork muttered. As near as he could tell, though, plan B simply meant they would leave the area with great haste!'"

"It still sounded mighty risky to Pork, but he agreed to give Weed the lead."

"'You just stand back and give me room and I'll show you how it's done.' Weed's bravado was betrayed somewhat by his quavering voice."

"An operation of this magnitude, though, could not just be rushed into. Some planning was required. Weed's consisted of backing off about twenty yards and beginning a series of exercises to loosen up. He did a few side-straddle hops and deep knee bends to stretch his muscles. He then assumed a yoga position, holding himself completely motionless for thirty seconds, before suddenly popping his eyes open and leaping into the air. At the same time, he began to mutter encouragement to himself. 'You can do this, you will do this!' he said repeatedly until, at least in *his* mind, he was ready."

"'OK, now stand back and watch the master operate,' he announced."

"Weed just oozed confidence. He grabbed the broom as near to the end as possible for maximum extension, then jabbed the air a couple of times to get the heft of the instrument. Next, he took a couple of dry runs close to the nest to gauge the distances involved, making sure he didn't prematurely disturb the insects who had begun to mill around nervously. Finally, convincing himself that he had done all he could to insure success, he launched the attack."

"Leaving his starting position from a track runner's crouch, he was off. His feet were a blur as he sped toward the target. He really was the fastest kid at school and he was confident his speed would serve him well. As it turned out, it became his enemy as he misjudged the timing of his leap, striking the eave of the house a foot past the target, jarring the broom from his hand. It fell to the ground directly below the nest, leaving him with nothing but wounded pride and a jammed wrist for his efforts. Two or three of the wasps had dropped off the nest, dive bombing his head as he flew by, but no damage was done."

" Of course, now he would have to retrieve the broom for another run. Pork advised him to wait a few minutes to allow the wasps to settle down. Their milling had become much more rapid and they were clearly uneasy about the unexpected intrusion into their sanctuary. Weed was not impressed."

"'Weed, you might ought to wait a minute and let 'em calm down a little," Pork advised.

"'Come on, Pork. Show a little back bone. I saw a bee keeper on TV last week pick up a cluster of bees in his hands and move 'em around like a wad of taffy. And he never got stung, neither. If he can do that, surely I can get that broom without any problem'"

"Weed was getting charged up now. The battle lines had been drawn and he knew that victory would not be achieved by the faint hearted. 'You just stand back a little while I get our broom back and we'll make quick work of this.'"

"Weed began a slow stalk toward the broom, going into a low crouch as he got closer. He was crawling on hands and knees by the time he was within five feet. The wasps were totally aware of the intruder and their milling grew faster and faster. A few of them even unlimbered their wings, producing a faint buzzing noise, which should have served as a warning."

"Weed ignored them. He now dropped to his belly and extended his body until it was stretched out to its maximum length for his final reach for the prize. He slithered forward a couple of more feet and was now within reach. The wasps' wings blurred as they revved their motors, the buzzing becoming louder by the second. Weed extended his long right arm and his hand closed on the broom handle. 'See, Pork. I told you. Nothin' to it,' was his triumphant proclamation as he drug the broom to him. Holding the handle tightly to his chest, he began to get to his feet."

"This must have been the signal for the wasps to put

their own plan into action. An angry red cloud dropped off the nest and surrounded his head, dive bombing it in clusters of two or three at a time, their stingers finding the mark with amazing accuracy. A fierce 'Rebel yell' erupted from Weed's prostrate figure, quickly followed by a miracle of levitation as Weed's body rose from the ground, the broom clenched firmly in hand. The rebel yells continued at a volume probably not heard since 'Pickett's Charge.'"

"His odds might have been better at that event than they were now. As the angry horde circled his head, he began swinging the broom like a batter at batting practice, only much faster."

"Not that Pork was witnessing the spectacle, though. With Weed's first yell, Pork had retreated to a safe spot on the other side of the house. He did not have to see Weed to know what was happening, though. The sounds told the story as well as his eyes could have. In between the intermittent yells, which had now deteriorated to pathetic gurgling sobs, he could hear a steady WHOOSH… WHOOSH as the broom was wielded with maximum effort but little effect. In between the WHOOSHES could now be heard 'Bronx cheers' as wasp after wasp penetrated his defenses and found footholds on Weed's lips. Each was blown off by saliva laden gusts of air but not before injecting his potent venom into Weed's lips."

"In only a few minutes, the battle was over, Weed weighing the relative merits of acquiring fish bait to that of continuing his life and deciding the latter was infinitely more appealing. Giving up the broom, he began raking the beasts off his face with his bare hands. At the same time, he began a headlong flight toward sanctuary without benefit of actually seeing his flight path."

"Directly in front of him was a set of patio furniture arranged about a circular wooden table with a huge, open beach umbrella in the middle. He crashed full tilt into this collection, first tripping on a lawn chair which folded up around his leg, spinning him backwards and depositing his rear end upon the table, the umbrella abruptly snapping shut, imprisoning him within its spindly grasp. As he began exploring avenues of escape, he was jabbed fiercely by the wires previously supporting the canopy. Several of the wasps were trapped within the enclosure with him and continued their relentless onslaught."

"Pork had finally stopped running and looked warily around the corner of the house. Not spotting Weed, he assumed he had escaped around the opposite side of the house. Then he noticed a couple of mangled chairs and a giant umbrella lying on the ground with a pair of scrawny legs sticking out."

"Moving in that direction, he began hearing muffled screams laced with insults issuing from within. 'Pork, you chicken livered, lard butt. Drag your cowardly carcass over here and get me outta here.'"

"Had he wanted to, which he did not, Pork could not have helped. He was rolling on the ground, laughing enough to bring tears. He was so weak, he could hardly stand, much less help his friend."

"As he gathered his faculties, he began making feeble efforts to free Weed. As the last spindle was folded back and Weed turned to face him, Pork gasped at the apparition confronting him. Weeds lips reminded him of a couple of wieners laid horizontally on one another, centered on his face below his nose. His eyes were swollen almost completely shut and his nose did a pretty fair Emmett Kelly impression. Little red dots were scattered about the remainder of his face, testifying to the numerous direct hits achieved by his tormentors. 'Oh, my God!', Pork shrieked as Weed's face emerged into clear view. He began another round of laughter, but quickly stifled it as he saw that Weed was on the verge of tears. Pork could manage only a weak protest even as Weed again took up the broom and began thrashing him with it."

"Unfortunately for poor Weed, his ordeal was only half over. Hearing the screams from her patio, his mother had demanded that he get into the house where she soundly doused him with her pet cure for every ailment: liberal amounts of alcohol. His screams could be heard for two blocks, even over the forlorn scraping sound of Pork's bicycle, as it slowly made its way back homeward, before any explanations were demanded of him."

"Pork was resigned to the fact that on this day, things were not destined to work out. It wasn't long after that experience that Pork and Weed discovered that fire was just the thing for convincing angry wasps to give up their homes in favor of their lives. A quick swipe with a wad of flaming newspapers tied onto a long stick eliminated all but the most agile of the swarming insects, which quickly buzzed away, leaving their nest unprotected to be plucked like a ripe apple. With that discovery, they never had much trouble with wasps again, but other problems soon arose. Pork set his dad's barn on fire twice before Mr. Campbell told him if he ever caught him with another match, he'd set Pork's pants on fire. And I don't think he intended to use a match, either."

"Pork was like that. Fishing was his passion and very

little could deter him from that pursuit. I guess we were all kinda like that in those days, not having much else to occupy our time. I think you kids have got a little of it in your blood, too, don't ya'll?'

"Yessir, I think you're right," Rod agreed. "but Gramps, did they ever get that fishing trip in?"

"Not that day, Rod, but they didn't have long to wait before they got to go."

"It was Weed's misfortune to have remarkable regenerative powers. He was able to keep his mother's sympathy for only a couple of days before she pronounced him well enough to return to normal activities, especially church. In spite of his protestations, he was decked out in his Sunday finery and paraded into his Sunday School class as calm and cool as you please. His classmates all turned into instant comedians."

"'Hey, Weed, did you win the ice pick fight?'"

"'Hey Weed. Did you get the number of that truck?'"

"'Hey Weed. Are measles contagious?'"

"To his credit, he took it all in stride, never giving them the satisfaction of hearing him whine. He knew that the final outcome would only enhance his reputation as the most fearless of the fearless. The outcome was so positive, he would have almost been willing to go through the ordeal again. Almost."

"Well, anyway, the most important thing is that they weren't hurt seriously," chimed in Elly.

"Well, that's a mighty considerate attitude which will come in real handy if you think you're going to be a nurse someday, Elly," Gramps said.

Elly glowed at this compliment. Nursing was what she had always wanted to do, even at this early age.

" I want to be a fisherman, Gramps," Rod told him.

"That's an admirable ambition, too," said Gramps, " but it may be a little harder to make a living at. But I will say, you sure seem to have it in your blood. And you could do worse. You could sure do a lot worse."

Chapter 4
The Fish Bait Business

The old man had once again taken his accustomed position in the hammock and with his audience of two, began to reminisce about his boyhood. After hearing the story about the best bream bait being wasp larvae, Rod said he had been told by one of his uncles that red wigglers were much better and that crickets were even better. Gramps allowed as how "They're pretty good, I guess but we didn't have money for either one when I was young, so we had to find our own. You might find a cricket here and there if you picked up enough pieces of board, but it was a spotty method at best. And I ain't ever seen a red wiggler in the wild. They must grow 'em up north somewheres."

"Well, if you couldn't buy them, what did you do for worms, Gramps?" Rod asked.

"I know where there's a bunch of worms," Ellie announced. "Under the edge of the house where Gramma's sink drain leaks."

"Well, I see my secret worm bed is no longer a secret," said Gramps. "Yep, there's a bunch of worms there, but not red wigglers. Big ole swamp wigglers is what we call 'em. Real good for bedding bass and the best catfish bait there is. 'Cept maybe for chicken livers."

Gramp's mind was drifting back to the summer that he and Weed Wilkins and Pork Campbell had discovered the secret of finding worms and the unfortunate incident which followed.

"Well, it wasn't too long after our encounter with the wasp colony that we found out about gruntin' for worms. This consisted of finding a likely looking spot and driving a stick into the ground and then rubbing a board across the top of the stick. This procedure apparently set up some sort of vibration the worms didn't like and they'd swarm to the top and we'd scoop them up and put them in a bucket. We'd keep enough for ourselves and sell the extras to the rich kids in town. We made a pretty good little piece of change, too. Then we got greedy. We'd been in business a couple of weeks when Pork called one day, all excited about a new way he said he'd found to gather worms. We told him to come on over and show us since gruntin' was kinda dirty and tiresome."

"Me and Weed were actually gruntin' for worms, down on our hands and knees, rootin' around like a couple of old hogs when Pork lumbered up. He was carrying something which looked like an old telephone with a couple of long wires attached."

"'Ya'll can waller 'round in the mud all day if you want to,' he says, ' but I've done found an easier way,' he announced."

" I can't say we were enjoying our way very much so we decided to at least listen to Pork's plan."

"'Well, Mr. Champeen Worm Digger, why don't you tell us what that thing is. Anyway, my momma says my fingernails are gonna fall off if I get any more dirt under them.' Weed was always supportive of new ideas."

"'That's the beauty of my plan,' Pork said. 'With this device you'll be able to pick the worms up right off the top of the ground. My Uncle Speck says he's done it many times'"

"'Well, talk is cheap', Weed spat. 'Let's see it work.'"

"'Just be patient, guys,' Pork instructed. He was not one to be rushed when he had the spotlight. 'Ya'll will see all in good time. First we gotta find us a good damp place sure to have plenty of worms to test it right. Skid, I think the best place is your momma's old sink drain. There's always plenty of worms there.'"

"You see, Ellie, that drains been producing worms for two generations."

"'Yeah, it's a good place alright,' she said. "But my mama's done told me she don't want me diggin' under there no more 'cause it just leaves a big hole for water to gather in and for 'skeeters to breed in.'"

"That's true Ellie, " Gramps admitted, "but in those days we didn't pay much attention to the advice of grown-ups. Maybe that's why we got into so much trouble."

"But as we will see, Pork was undaunted. 'No problem', he said. 'This system don't require any digging. Come on, I'll show you how easy it is.' It was useless to try and stop him once he set his mind and we were tired of digging anyway, so we followed along behind."

"When we arrived, Pork set the telephone device down and began to explain how it worked. 'You see,' he began, 'This old phone contains an electric generator. When you crank this handle real fast, it produces an electric current which travels through these two wires which we then stick into the ground. The worms don't care much for getting' shocked so they crawl out of the ground to escape the electricity. They are 'shocked' up to the top. All we have to do then is pick 'em up. Any questions? Speck promised it works great. And my aunt says he ain't lied hardly at all since he was paroled last year."

"It sounded simple enough to actually work, so we agreed to give it a try."

"'Great,' said Pork. 'Now here's what we'll do. I'll crawl up under the house where the ground's the wettest and plug these wires into the ground. When I give the signal, Weed, you turn the crank as fast as you can. Skid, you bring the bucket and all we gotta do is pick 'em up.'"

"Pork took one end of a wire in each hand and began crawling. The space was just high enough to allow Pork to crawl on his hands and knees causing him to keep bumping his head and scraping his back. Even so, he reached his destination without mishap. By leaning down, we could just make out his bulk wedged back into a corner where the leaky pipe was located. He hunched up onto his knees, looking for all the world like a huge toad frog. He jabbed the two wires into the ground but they had retained their 'memory', having been coiled up for some time and immediately popped out."

"'Aw, heck, I guess I'll have to hold them in place,' he muttered as he wrapped one wire around each wrist to keep them from slipping and jammed the ends into the ground. The ground literally squished each time he moved, indicating that it was very moist indeed. 'The ground's really wet,' he announced. 'That out to give us a real good connection. OK, boys, I'm ready. Give it a good crank.'"

"Weed put his whole body into it, rapidly cranking it several revolutions. This action was accompanied by a soft whirring noise as the generator turned, then a sharp crackling, popping noise from under the house. Suddenly, there was a bear-like bellow from Pork, who was receiving the full charge of the current. 'Good God-A-Mighty!' he screamed. 'Eeeeeeeyowwwwww' was the last sound we heard before he somehow got his feet underneath him and shot straight up between two floor joists. The electrodes seemed to be stuck to his hands as rapid and violent shaking failed to dislodge them."

"Oblivious to Pork's yelling and frantic gyrations, Weed was still cranking like a demon. I guess he thought that was part of the plan of scaring the worms to the top. Pork had had enough. With a mighty effort, he stood up, his head striking the kitchen floor, which had been weakened by steady rot over the years. His head broke through right under my momma's feet as she stood in front of the sink washing dishes."

"Her surprise at suddenly having a screaming head on the floor between her feet was exceeded only by the volume of her own screams which, when added to those of Pork, created a racket closely resembling that produced by two panthers screeching."

"She levitated off the floor, dropping the cast iron skillet she had been scrubbing. A loud 'CLANG' announced its contact with Pork's already throbbing head, knocking him temporarily senseless. My dad, who had been painting the front porch, came flying into the room, colliding with Momma, who was just as quickly flying out."

"She was hysterical. 'Abner, Abner,' she cried, the pitch of her voice reaching new levels, 'There's someone coming up through the floor! Stop him, Stop him!'"

"Dad, being a man of action, took one look, saw the unidentified head sticking through the floor and screamed, 'Alright, you creep, I'll teach you to look up my wife's dress!.'"

"This warning was followed by several quick slaps to the protruding head with the only thing available to him at the time, a wet paint brush loaded with red paint."

"Pork began to regain his faculties by this time and made a valiant effort to dodge the blows, snapping his head from side to side as each blow connected."

"Weed and I came running into the kitchen and were greeted by a scene too bizarre to imagine: a balding, middle-aged man, clad only in Bermuda shorts and flip flops, frantically slapping at a wildly thrashing head with a paint brush, both of them screaming obscenities and each trying his best to override the hysterical screams of the distraught woman in the background.

"'DAD! IT'S PORK!!,' I yelled. 'Stop. You're killin' him!'"

"Not hearing my voice as it was drowned out by so much other noise, he kept right on slapping. Weed and I, realizing the futility of voice commands, each grabbed an arm and drug him off."

"Poor Pork looked like the latest victim in a horror movie. Several cuts were oozing blood, which was indistinguishable from the bright red paint from Dad's brush."

"'Thank the Lord ya'll showed up,' Pork said to Weed and me. 'I thought I was gonna be painted to death!'"

"This episode put a quick end to our bait selling business. What little money we had made was required to repair the floor and Dad made us fix the leaky pipe for good measure. Speck reclaimed his generator from Pork but he soon lost it again after getting caught shocking fish in the river."

"Gramps, I'm sure glad there are bait stores we can

use today and we don't have to catch our own," Rod spoke.

"Me, too," said Ellie.

"Yeah, I guess so," said Gramps. "Still, it makes you appreciate it more if you have to work at it a little," he allowed as he spat a stream of tobacco juice into a can on the ground. Ya'll come on. Let's go see what Gramma's got cookin'."

Chapter 5
The Cat's Big Arm

"Hey, you kids come here a minute," Gramps called out as Rod and Ellie emerged from Gramma's car.

They were returning from a shopping trip to get them new tennis shoes. This was an annual event and much anticipated by the kids. Not only did they get new shoes, Gramma always took them for hamburgers and a milkshake, afterwards.

They spied Gramps ambling toward his hammock, just having finished his favorite lunch, a tomato and mayonnaise sandwich loaded with salt and pepper. They came running up just as he reached his destination. Each wanted to be the first to show off their new shoes and neither would relinquish the spotlight long enough for the old man to perform a proper examination. After a few minutes of pushing and shoving, along with demands from each for the other to shut up, Gramps decided to settle the matter himself.

"Now just quiet down, the both of you," he commanded. Instant silence followed. "A body cain't hear himself think with all that commotion goin' on. Now, Rod, it's about time you began learning how a gentleman's supposed to act. It ain't always a competition, you know. Now, seeing as how Ellie's the youngest and a female to boot, it's just right for a gentleman to let her go first. So, you just hold on for a minute and then it'll be your turn, OK?"

Rod hesitantly nodded his head in the affirmative, although not totally convinced. He'd do it because Gramps asked him to but he still didn't like it. His disposition was not improved when Ellie stuck out her tongue at him and quipped, 'See, I told you; ladies are supposed to go first, Mr. Smarty!'

"Right, Ellie", Gramps broke in, "Ladies are supposed to be first, but they must remember to act like a lady. Your attitude's not one for a lady to have. When a gentleman is being courteous, you must learn to be gracious. Now, young lady, you owe Rod an apology."

"OK, Rod I'm sorry you're so crude," she retorted.

"That's not what I had in mind, Ellie, and you know it," Gramps gave her a stern look.

Her frown turned to her most charming smile as she cooed, "Oh, I <u>am</u> sorry, your highness." This was accompanied by an exaggerated bow. "I <u>do</u> hope you can forgive my ignorance. I wouldn't be able to <u>live</u> without your approval." This was followed by her breaking into an uncontrollable giggling fit. Rod glared but said nothing.

"OK, OK, that's enough etiquette for today," Gramps conceded defeat. "I'll just sit here and admire both pairs of shoes at the same time. He grabbed one foot of each child and dragged them into the hammock, making an exaggerated examination of each foot at close range. "Yessir, them's some nice ones", he said. Both children now broke into giggles, forgetting their confrontation of a few minutes earlier.

"Now, you kids sit down over there so I can tell you about something funny that happened in church last Sunday." They obediently took their places and waited for the tale they were sure was coming.

"Now, that's more like it. It's hard for a man my age to gather his thoughts when there's too much distraction." They were used to his pretense of senility, although they knew he could keep up with most men half his age.

"Now, where was I? Oh, yeah, I was 'bout to tell ya'll about what the preacher said last Sunday. Old Reverend Hoover really stuck his foot in his mouth. "Course in his case, his foot would probably fit if he actually did put it in there. Remember, now, you don't have to repeat everything I say. He's a real nice fellow, I suppose, but he sure likes to eat and consequently looks sorta like a big ol' walrus. He's always first in line at homecoming dinner and usually makes several return trips. His excuse is that he don't want to offend the ladies, seeing as how they put so much preparation time into the meals."

"The Reverend's probably had a speech class or two and he knew that if you want to hold an audience's attention, you need to tell them a story or joke before they have a chance to tune you out. The Preacher began telling the congregation about a dog and cat fight he had witnessed the week before. 'It was a Jim Dandy of a fight,' he said. Most everyone had already heard about it from their neighbors but they figured that if the preacher wanted to tell it again, they wouldn't disappoint him. Anyway, he was a bona-fide eye witness, the ruckus having started in the vacant lot right in front of the parsonage as he sat on his veranda sipping tea and fanning himself with a hand-held fan."

"'What happened,' Reverend Hoover continued,' was that old Jake Brenner's fox hound, Jeb, had gotten out of his pen and was roamin' the neighborhood, looking for something to chase. Since there ain't many foxes in town,

Jeb had to settle for whatever he could find, which in this case was the Widder Fincher's prize Persian, Cleo. Jeb spied Cleo just as her and the Widder was turning onto her walkway at the conclusion of their morning walk. He began howling as soon as he saw the white puff of fur tied to the Widder's arm and made a beeline straight for the terrified creature.'"

"'Cleo had gotten pretty excited at the first howls coming from Jeb's direction. Her excitement now turned to panic as she saw him coming at her full tilt, teeth bared and drool flying. She assumed the universal fightin' cat posture, fur standing straight up, back arched, alternately hissing and spitting from between her own bared teeth. Miss Fincher, poor soul, didn't realize what was happening until it was way too late.'"

"'Cleo made a short run, but was snatched back into the fray as soon as she ran out of leash. At that instant, she was bowled over by the snarling, howling hound. She quickly regained her balance and began dancing around on her hind legs, clawing at Jeb's face to keep him at bay.'"

"'But Jeb was determined to get at his quarry and began a series of quick, darting movements in between flurries of cat claws and swipes from the Widder's cane. Cleo, realizing her only hope was flight, began running in ever diminishing circles as the leash wrapped around Miss Fincher's ankles. The old lady was now screeching like a banshee, still trying her best to brain the dog with her cane. After a few turns of the leash, she was immobilized and began wobbling like a bowling pin, finally toppling over in a heap on top of Cleo who was snugged up tight against her legs.'"

"'For a few short seconds, the tangled mass of

humanity and cat fur looked some kind of monster in its final death throes. Sensing the kill, Jeb sailed in for the *coup de grace*. Fortunately for all, at that instant the leash broke. Out of the mass shot a white blur, a brown and black blur only inches behind.'"

"The Preacher was really hittin' his stride now, his voice booming, 'As they left Miss Fincher's yard, they crossed my lawn only a few yards from where I sat. Well, brethren and ladies the cat run up my chinaberry tree and just knew she had reached safety.' His booming voice got louder still, 'That ole cat just lay out on a limb, a smug expression on her face as the frantic dog jumped and howled for all he was worth. The disinterested cat just continued licking and smoothing her fur. The dog would run up the tree trunk a few feet and jump as high as he could, snapping and howling all the while. The cat showed not a care in the world as she continued contentedly grooming herself. This went on for a good while and by this time Miss Fincher had extricated herself from the leash and gone into the house to call for help. Old Jeb's jumping and howling finally wore him out and after a few more half hearted leaps, he turned and began trotting off to look for new quarry.'"

"'All of a sudden, 'KEEERACK!' went the limb as it broke. It and the attached cat came crashing to the ground. Jeb immediately resumed his mission with renewed vigor. He was on the cat quicker than you could say spit. In a flash, they came right by me, the cat in the lead but not by more than a hair, both of them doing ninety or nothing.' "The congregation was really getting into the story and sat spell-bound, their attention riveted on the preacher. This just seemed to spur him on. He bellowed even louder, 'An I tell you, brothers and sisters,

THAT CAT'S ARM WAS AS BIG AS MY TAIL!!!' The preacher continued his tale, getting more and more animated as it unfolded. As he paused for breath, he noticed the first couple of restrained snickers. "

"A moment of complete silence ensued before a few more isolated snickers began bursting forth from throughout the gathering. Then a few giggles could be heard. No one wanted to admit what they were thinking. He did, after all, have an ample derriere. Then the uncontrollable disease of suppressed laughter broke out all over the place. Parishioners who hadn't had a good laugh in months became red-faced with the effort of trying to hold it in. None who had caught the error could hold it in any longer, many faces streaked with tears."

"Preacher Hoover, after a short pause had continued on with the story, concluding it with the cat making its escape through the little pet door Miss Fincher had installed for Cleo's benefit. As he gazed around the room, he began to wonder why everyone was teary eyed and looking everywhere but at him. Though he knew the story was funny, he thought there was way too much laughter to be attributed solely to its telling. So, now he stopped and with a befuddled look on his face asked, 'Did I miss something, brethren?' Whatever laughter had gone before was now doubled. The Preacher remained dumbfounded."

"Finally, the Chairman of Deacons, a brave soul by the name of Elijah Haines, stood. Barely suppressing a grin, he sheepishly asked, 'Now jest how big did you say that cat's ARM was, Preacher?'"

"All restraints were now broken as an unrestrained eruption of laughter burst forth. Reverend Hoover's face turned beet red, his embarrassment total. But, being a good sport and accustomed to being the butt of jokes, he broke out in a huge grin. 'Well, I guess it was pretty dang big!' he allowed. A sea of nodding heads emphatically agreed".

"The reverend finally regained enough composure to deliver his sermon but I don't believe anyone heard a word of it that day. Stifled snickers punctuated his speech as first one, then another lost control during the remainder of the sermon."

Gramps finished with a big grin on his own face. "Now you young'uns don't need to say anything about it when the Preacher comes around to dinner next week, you hear."

"Why not, Gramps?" they chorused.

"Because," Gramps explained, "You never know when you may need a good man of God and you don't want him holding no grudges." Gramps believed in covering all the angles.

Chapter 6
Dog Tails

It was the second week of Rod and Ellie's summer visit to the farm when a neighbor, Charlie Roach called and said he had heard the grandkids were there and wanted to stop by and give them a present. Charlie was one of Gramps' oldest friends and even though he had been known to pull a practical joke or two, Gramps didn't think he would pull anything on the kids. Charlie wouldn't tell what the gift was as he didn't want to spoil the surprise and wanted to personally witness their reactions.

The children had heard Mr. Charlie was coming over with something for them and could hardly contain their excitement as they waited on the front porch. Gramps knew Charlie well enough to have some vague misgivings about anything he was willing to give away. He was known as being somewhat tight-fisted, so Gramps figured anything he would give away would probably not be worth having. Well, he reasoned, if it would make Charlie happy, he wouldn't forbid it. He could always make some excuse to the kids for Charlie's frugal nature.

An hour later, their vigil was rewarded as they spied Charlie's old pickup slowly bumping its way up the drive. As the truck neared the house, Rod and Ellie began jumping up and down and squealing. Gramps just snorted and told them to "quit acting like dern fools."

Charlie's face was fixed in a huge grin as he brought the old heap to a grinding halt and climbed out. "Hey, Mr. Charlie, what you got for us?" Ellie asked first, followed quickly by Rod's similar inquiry, each child imagining some great treasure, Ellie's thoughts running towards a new doll or maybe a dress. Rod's imaginings included fishing poles, ball gloves and Barlow knives."

"Not so fast, kids." Charlie cautioned. He was being coy. He opened the truck door and began a slow, methodical search, pretending he could not find the treasure he was seeking. "Now, I know them things are here somewhere," he said with his most forlorn look. "Maybe Nell forgot to put them in the truck." The children's faces fell at this pronouncement and Charlie could tease them no more. "Oh, here they are," he said as he produced two K-Mart bags, handing one to each child. Rob's bag contained a plastic slingshot. Ellie's held a Raggedy Ann doll. Just as Gramps had suspected, the gifts were very inexpensive. Even so, the kids had been taught to show their gratitude even in small things and thanked Mr. Charlie for his thoughtfulness. "I thought you'd like 'em," was all he said.

Gramps was disappointed, too, but Charlie was an old friend and he would not be rude. "Why don't you come in and set a spell, Charlie," he invited.

"Why, thank you kindly, Skid, but the wife's waitin' supper for me, so I better get goin'."

He began to walk around the rear of his truck when his elbow struck the tailgate, which promptly fell open with a loud clunk, revealing a card-board box in the truck bed. Soft whimpering sounds accompanied by loud scratching noises could be heard coming from the box.

"Why, what have we here?" Charlie feigned surprise at the box's presence. He slid it off the tailgate tilting it onto its side just as it reached the ground. Out tumbled two brown balls of fur, which sprouted legs and began leaping on Rod and Ellie, giving them each a good face licking. Each of the puppies was quickly scooped up and hugged to a child's breast. "Well, would you look at that, Skid. Have you ever seen puppies take to children as quick as those two?"

"Oh, they're so cute," Ellie shrieked. 'Just look at that fuzzy little face! Aren't they the sweetest things?"

Gramps was too busy glaring at Charlie to notice how "cute" the puppies were, knowing the battle was already lost.

"Mighty careless of you to knock that tailgate open, don't you think?" accused Gramps.

"Well, I been meaning to get that thing fixed, but just ain't got around to it. You know how it is," Charlie explained.

"Yeah, I think I understand completely, Roach. I hope you brought some blindfolds for the kids 'cause they ain't used to seein' me whale the tar out of people right in front of 'em."

"Now, Skid, calm down. If you say they can't keep 'em, I'll take 'em right home."

Charlie, too, knew the battle was over.

That was confirmed as Rod and Ellie began their pleas, "Please, Gramps, can't we keep 'em? You been saying we need a watch dog. Can we keep 'em? Pleeeasse!"

Even though he knew the game was over, he still wanted to lay down some ground rules while he had the chance. "Well, we might consider it if you agree to certain conditions."

"Oh, we know we'll have to feed 'em and water 'em and clean up after 'em," Rod assured him. "We've got no problem with that."

"That's a good beginning, but that ain't all," Gramps said. "You've also got to keep them bathed and provide flea and tick medicine. And they're not staying in the house."

"We'll do whatever it takes," Ellie chimed in.

"OK, kids. It might do you good to learn some responsibility. I guess you can keep 'em. But I warn you, if you don't take care of them, we'll find a new home for 'em right away."

"Don't worry, we'll take good care of 'em." Both kids were adamant.

"Sure, I'll bet," Gramps said. "Now be sure and thank Mr. Cockroach, er Mr. Roach."

They each heaped a dozen "thankyous" on Mr. Roach before they rushed in to show their prizes to Gramma. A loud shriek was heard, followed by the slamming of the back door as Gramma shooed them right on out onto the back porch. Gramps could hear her muttering, "Dern old fool! He knows better'n to let them young'uns keep some flea-bitten hounds. Ain't got the sense God promised a billy goat!"

Gramps knew he was going to catch it when company left. He took Roach by the elbow and led him to the truck. "You know, Roach, things have got a way of evenin' out in the long run, so you better keep your eyes open. Ain't no man yet got the best of Will Skidmore and I don't 'spect you'll be the first."

"Aw, Skid. Them kids love those pups and I still got six more to get rid of. You oughta be thankin' me instead of threatening me."

"Thanking you! I oughta throttle you. What kinda mutts are they anyway?"

"Near as I can figure, they're a cross between a shepherd and a chow. I ain't real sure, though, what with dogs running around loose everywhere, you know."

"That figures. You couldn't give me something small, could you? Do you have any idea how much them things are gonna eat? You might oughta get out of here before I change my mind."

"But you already told the kids they could keep the pups," Charlie reminded him.

"I ain't talkin' about keepin' the dogs," Gramps roared. "I'm talking about throttling you!"

"Oh," Charlie said weakly as he got into the truck. "I guess I'm outta here. Wife's waitin' supper. Enjoy the dogs."

Gramps felt sure he heard a soft chuckle as Charlie drove off. "Well, what's done is done'" he thought to himself.

He ambled around the side of the house and found Rod and Ellie playing with the pups in the grass in the shade of the pecan tree.

"Hi, Gramps," Ellie chirped. "Meet Lady. Rod's puppy is named Ruff."

"Lord help me, they've named 'em already," he moaned. "Ain't no gettin' rid of them now."

"They're the best puppies ever, Gramps. Thank you for getting' them for us."

"They even think the puppies were my idea," he signed. "Well, since we're stuck with 'em, I might as well enjoy the credit, at least from the kids," he thought to himself. "'Cause I'm sure gonna get the blame from

Gramma."

"Aw, I just figured it's about time you kids learned something about responsibility. Caring for an animal is as good a way as any, I reckon."

He caught Rod winking at Ellie and had the vaguest notion he was being manipulated. He shrugged it off and continued. "First thing is, they're your dogs. Not mine. Not Gramma's. That means caring for them every day, not just when you feel like it. For the first month or two, they're going to be just like a couple of babies, so you might as well get ready for it."

"Don't worry, Gramps," Rod assured him. "We know what we have to do and we intend to do it."

"Spoken like a man, son. But good intentions don't mean a thing unless they're followed by actions. Time will tell."

Later that afternoon, after the pups were fed and were fast asleep, Gramps and the children found their usual spots under the shade of the pecan trees. The heat was oppressive as usual. Lemonade had magically appeared from Gramma's kitchen and each of them held a cold glass, sipping sparingly to make it last.

Rod and Ellie were still pretty excited about their new playmates. No matter how much Gramps told them about their awesome "responsibility", their enthusiasm remained high. Encouraged by their demeanor, Gramps decided that he would adopt a more positive attitude himself. "You know," he said, "I've had some pretty crazy experiences with dogs myself over the years. They can be crazy animals at times. Of course, they can be a big pain at times, too, but on balance, I'd say you're better off with 'em than without 'em in the long run."

"What kind of dogs did you have?" Ellie asked. Rod's

eyes told the old man he'd like to know, too.

"Well, there's been quite a variety over the years, but one which seems to stand out was a collie dog named Rory owned by my old friend Weed Wilkins. I remember one particular run-in Rory had with my old friend Pork."

Gramps paused at this point to light his pipe, sending a cloud of blue smoke into the air. Then he proceeded to blow a series of small smoke rings, one following the other, the latter ones floating through the expanding holes in the previous ones. This always amazed the kids. He admonished them, that smoking was not a good habit to acquire and that he had been trying to give it up for years"

"Back to the story," he said. "Pork had brought an oscillating fan over to the Wilkins' house, returning it after some minor repair or other. Rory was sitting in front of Weed on the porch getting his ears scratched, when Pork arrived with the fan. He announced that his dad had fixed it but he better plug it in just to be sure it was working properly. As Pork inserted the cord into the receptacle, the fan whirred to life and began its slow, back and forth swings. Pork set it down on the porch so all could enjoy its cool breeze. His mistake in setting it too close to Rory soon became very evident."

"On about the third or forth swing, the fan's blades intercepted Rory's slowly swishing, shaggy tail. It was immediately and quite rudely snatched into the blades, setting up the wildest commotion seen on the back porch since Grandpa sat on the cat. Rory jumped up and began spinning in circles, howling like a coyote, snarling and snapping at the "monster" which was pulling the hair off his tail. Unfortunately, he never moved far enough to pull the plug which would have ended his ordeal."

“Instead, every turn of the fan blade wound his tail hair tighter around the shaft, all the while beating the meaty part of his tail with the edges of the blades. Not able to extricate his tail, Rory did what any dog would have done: he bit the cord. This produced a crackling sound accompanied by a few sparks and a puff of smoke.”

“Rory leaped off the porch at full speed, the fan in tow, the cord trailing closely behind. Pork made a grab for the fan, barely missing it, but snaring the cord just as the unfortunate dog came to the end of the slack. He was brought to an abrupt halt, much like a roped calf, his tail still firmly captured by the fan blades. As he was turning to face his attacker, the first thing he saw was Pork, still holding the source of his suffering in his hand.”

“His mind instantly reached an unmistakable conclusion: Pork was the cause of his pain and thus was his enemy! Forgetting for a moment that he was a collie dog, generally known to be gentle and friendly to humans, Rory decided to seek his revenge then and there. Baring his teeth, he came at Pork, snarling like a wolf. Pork began a crab-like retreat in reverse, not daring to turn his back on the snapping jaws. His heels struck the bottom step, stopping the progress of his feet but not that of his upper body. He toppled over backwards, landing on his back, feet in the air, arms flailing wildly. His screams shattered the stillness of the quiet neighborhood. ‘Goda’mighty, Weed,’ he screamed. ‘Grab him, grab him!’”

“Weed was already moving, leaping off the porch and tackling Rory, taking him down a foot short of his goal. He and Rory rolled over a couple of times, wrapping the cord tightly around themselves.”

“’Nice tackle, Weed. You saved my life,’ was all Pork could think to say.”

“’Shut up, Pork,’ Weed shouted. ‘I probably just killed my dog and I’m not sure trading his life for yours would be such a good swap.’ Rory was far from dead, though. He had merely had the breath knocked out of him. Even immobilized as he was, he still snapped and snarled at the sight of Pork.”

“’Well, I gotta go,’ Pork announced. ‘Lots of chores to do you know,’ he excused himself as he edged closer to his bike. ‘Hope your mom enjoys the fan.’”

“’Sure, Pork, you run along now. I don’t know how much longer I can hold Rory, anyway,’ Weed agreed. ‘He’s gonna be awful mad when I turn him loose.’”

“’See ya’ll tomorrow,’ Pork called over his shoulder as he mounted his bike and rattled out of the yard.”

“It took Weed and his father most of the evening, using scissors and pliers, to free Rory’s tail, which afterward resembled that of a ‘possum. If dogs can be embarrassed, Rory was. With his full, luxurious tail, he had considered himself, top dog in the neighborhood. Now his beauty was marred. He spent the next few weeks skulking underneath the house, slinking out only long enough to eat, then quickly retiring to lick his wounds and salve his wounded ego, while waiting for his tail to be restored. Rory had remained Pork’s enemy ever since.”

“What about the other dogs ya’ll had?” Rod piped up.

“Well, let’s see, now, Gramps responded. “Seems like every dog we ever had was peculiar in some way or other. One pup we had loved to nurse an old momma cat. Every time Kitty would lay down, that pup was at her. That went on for a solid month until the day the pup chomped Kitty's milk bottle with his little needle sharp teeth. She sprang up and began hissin' and then raked his nose with her claws. The pup yelped like he'd been stuck with a hot poker and tore out of the yard, tail tucked tightly underneath. After that, he sorta lost his appetite for cat milk."

"We had one dog who had two injured feet, both on the same side. Didn't bother him none. He hopped around on his two good legs, just like that was his normal way. His sense of balance was amazing. I always wondered what he'd of done if one more foot got injured. It wouldn't have surprised me at all if he'd of hopped around on one foot."

"We had everything from Peek-a-poos to Bassett hounds plus some whose ancestry could not be determined, but they were all special in some way."

"We had a Beagle who almost choked to death on chicken skins my momma threw out and was rescued only by my dad, who improvised an early version of the Heimlich Maneuver. We had a Cocker Spaniel who loved to eat bananas. We had a Rat Terrier who was the best squirrel dog I ever saw. She was so cold natured, she would have to be kept inside your coat while waiting for a squirrel to show, but once she sighted one, he had no chance of eluding her keen eyesight, no matter how many trees he leaped into.

We had a black lab who was the smartest dog of them all. She learned tricks as fast as my dad could teach them to her and, once she learned them, she never forgot.

"We had a Great Dane whose only claim to fame was her immense size. She stood over six feet standing on her hind legs, but was gentle as a lamb. We kept a pack of Beagles which we fed year 'round, just to enjoy a couple of months of rabbit hunting with them. We could never keep them in their pen, they were such great diggers, so many a night was spent walking around in the woods, trying to convince them to leave the track and come on back home."

"We had a Pekingese, whose demeanor was sweeter than honey. She thought we were her humans, rather than her being our dog. It was one of the saddest days in the life of our family, when she ran in front of a car and had her short life snuffed out prematurely. There was Melvin, the neighborhood dog, who belonged to no one but was claimed by everyone. There were many more but these are the ones which come to mind at this moment. Our lives were enriched by each in his own way"

"Oh yeah, I almost forgot. My uncle Roscoe had a bird dog once who he called 'Esso' which he explained was the short version of this real name which was S.O.B. This was the most hyper mass of dog flesh I've ever seen and Roscoe had tried everything he could think of to gain some control, without much success. He'd brag anytime he was able to teach Esso anything which was rare indeed. That dog must have been on pep pills or something, the way he was constantly bouncing around. They did manage to bag a quail now and then, though, and he would fetch it, so Esso was allowed to remain."

"One day Uncle Roscoe invited me to go on a bird hunt with him and Esso. I knew he only invited me along so he'd have somebody to tramp through the thickest briar patches and flush out the birds which Esso would not go into. Esso was apparently not as stupid as he acted."

"As we were getting our guns and gear loaded into his old huntin' car, Uncle Roscoe motioned for me to come around to the back of the car."

"'Watch this, son,' he said as he reached for the latch to pop open the trunk. As soon as the trunk opened, Esso leaped in with a very 'eager to please' look on his face."

"'Good dog, Esso,' Roscoe fairly radiated pride as he turned and beamed at me. Then he turned back to the dog and issued another command, 'Out boy, Out.' Esso obediently leaped back to the ground."

"'Well, what do ya' think of that, boy?' Uncle Roscoe crowed. 'Only took me two days to learn him that.'"

"I got to admit,' I told Roscoe, "I think it'll be much nicer with him in the trunk. Esso had a notoriously weak stomach, bladder and bowels. He would almost always manage to deposit something or other on the back seat during the course of a trip."

"'Yep, I couldn't afford to keep puttin' new slip covers on after every trip so I had to do something. Besides your Aunt Ethel has a contract on his life if she ever catches him in the car again. Seems she left her pocketbook in the car and went to look for it before I could warn her that we'd been huntin' that mornin'. Well, she found it alright. It was just the sort of container Esso had needed when he got rid of his morning breakfast. Last I saw of her, she was two steps behind a streaking blur of bird dog, swinging the pocketbook like a cat-o-nine-tails, calling him by his full name and him howling with each contact of the pocketbook with his hindquarters'"

"Roscoe was proud of his progress with Esso's training and showed me the same trick a couple more times to convince me it was no fluke. It was evident Esso was tiring of this game and was ready to go. I told Uncle Roscoe I was impressed and suggested we get going."

"'OK, boy,' Uncle Roscoe announced, 'we're about

ready. I just need to adjust the idle screw. The engine's revvin' a little too high.'

"He cranked the car and sure enough, the motor did sound a little too fast. 'It'll just take a minute,' he said as he got out and raised the hood. In a flash Esso sprang into the engine compartment. Just as quickly he let out a yelp and leaped straight up, smashing his head on the hood. He then plunged back into the mass of whirling belts and pulleys, not to mention the mass of spark plug wires. I had not previously witnessed levitation, but Esso convinced me it was possible as he appeared to hover a few inches above the roaring engine. Each time a foot came down and contacted some moving part or wire, he picked it back up so fast he appeared to be floating in midair."

"'Gol dang fool dog,' Roscoe bellowed, 'the trunk's where you go!.' He made a couple of grabs at Esso's collar but was not quick enough. Finally, it dawned on him to cut the engine, which caused Esso to collapse in a heap on top of the motor. Roscoe grabbed a leg and drug him out, flopping him onto the ground, spread eagled. Esso was so glad to feel solid ground under his feet, I swear he kissed it. Needless to say, the day's trip was cancelled in favor of a trip to the vet to get Esso's injuries treated, not to mention the extensive cleanup required to rid the engine compartment of various bodily excretions deposited by Esso."

"Ole Esso was quite a character in other ways, too. Uncle Roscoe used to show off by soaking dinner napkins in gravy and tossing them to Esso, who would gobble them down like candy. One family member swore that he saw Roscoe tossing gravy soaked napkins to Esso one day and, as a joke, tossed him a new-born kitten which Esso gulped down without missing a beat. After being around that dog for a while, I wouldn't doubt it was true."

"Well, young'uns it's getting' on towards supper time…" Gramps began, then noticed that both children were sound asleep, each cradling a puppy in their arms. A twinkle or maybe it was a tear, came into his eye. "Well, now," he spoke softly to no one, I think they're gonna be all right. Yessir. All right."

Chapter 7
Fishing with Butch

"Did I ever tell you kids about the very first dog I ever had?"

Gramps was all excited. Or at least as excited as it was possible for a seventy-year old to get. The kids had had the pups three weeks now and far from being the nuisances he had anticipated, they had provided many hours of enjoyment for the family. Even Gramma had softened her attitude somewhat, although she still wouldn't allow them in the house. Lady and Ruff adored the children and tagged along behind them wherever they went. They were always ready for a wrestling match or a tug of war, using an old knotted rope which Gramps had produced.

Best of all, the kids had kept their promises to care for the pups, not missing a single feeding and cleaning up after them tirelessly. Gramps had devised what he termed a 'pooper scooper' which they used for the most onerous tasks. The children had become so enamored of their pets, Gramps had become a little jealous of all the attention they were getting.

He was determined not to lose his rightful place as the center of attention, though. He reverted to the only fool proof method he knew of. He decided it was time for a tale. The 'after lunch lull' seemed like the perfect time to do it.

“What dog was that, Gramps,” Rod asked. “ I thought you already told us about all your dogs.” Rod had been missing the story times they had become accustomed to and he encouraged his Grandfather to resume his practice.

“Not quite, my boy. I only told you about the later ones. This was one I had when I wasn’t much older than you are now. He was a black Cocker Spaniel, named Butch and as my first, he holds a special place in my heart. He taught me about loyalty and friendship at an early age. He would have followed me into a forest fire and not even hesitated. ‘Course, I’d a done the same for him too, I reckon.”

“We were each other’s best friends for many years. It’s kinda hard to see why, though, considering the rocky start we had.” Gramps paused to make sure he had their attention and took the opportunity to let loose a stream of tobacco juice into his ‘spit can’. “Bingo’” he exclaimed, notifying the world of his direct hit.

“So, what happened, Gramps?” Ellie was getting impatient.

“Just hold your pig tails there little girl. I’m getting’ to it. You cain’t rush a good tale any more you rush a good paintin’. You gotta get the mood just right, you know. Now where was I? Oh, yeah, me an’ old Butch got off on the wrong foot from the beginning but luckily, things got better later on. He was only about six months old and just full of vim and vigor. Couldn’t be still for a minute, bouncing around like he had springs in his feet.”

“Anyway, one bright spring day, I decided to take him on his first fishing trip.

At first light, we set off for Ashley’s pond, me on my old bike and Butch running alongside. Although a good five miles from my house, it was a mere stroll for Butch. He'd hardly even got warmed up by the time we arrived at the lake. He was running everywhere, sniffing at everything while I got the boat loaded. I gave a whistle and Butch came bounding out of the woods and raced over to me."

"'Come on, boy, jump in' I coaxed, but he was having none of that."

"He had never been in a boat and he wasn't planning on getting' in one that day either. The look on his face changed from 'all's right with the world' to one of sheer terror. Evidently, he thought his day could be better spent chasing woodland creatures than fishing. You never heard such whimpering and whining. He began to try to convince me that I should stay with him, rather than him go with me. He'd run up to the boat and stick his head over the side and then just as quickly jump back if I made any move to touch him."

"Well, the best fishing time was quickly getting away from me, a fact which was attested to by the whooping sound an unseen angler made as he boated a nice bass just up the shore. This only served to convince me that I didn't need to play games with a fool dog all day so I decided to resort to trickery."

"I'd brought along a couple of sandwiches for lunch so I extracted one from the paper sack and begun unwrapping it. Butch had learned very early, the meaning of the sound of wax paper unraveling, and his appetite for ham sandwiches betrayed him. His ears perked up and his mouth dropped open, saliva drooling. As he moved toward the sandwich, I slowly backed further into the boat and began easing us into the lake. He stepped cautiously into the boat and made a quick snapping motion, gobbling the sandwich down in one gulp. Having accomplished his goal, he made a hasty turn and started to jump out of the boat."

"His toenails made a screeching sound as he applied his brakes, noticing that we were now ten or fifteen feet off shore. He began barking and whining in earnest, hoping I would take him back in. I certainly had no intention of doing that. He calmed down after a few minutes, resigned to his fate and curled up on the bow seat, head resting on his paws, sad eyes looking at me accusingly. I figured 'What the heck. He's not bothering me.' So I let him stay where he was."

"I had brought along a fair collection of lures and I wanted to try them all. I wasn't fortunate enough to have a real tackle box in those days so I carried my tackle in an old cigar box. It did a fair job of keeping them together, but I spent half my time untangling the moment's lure of choice from the others in the clump. This was one of the rare days, my dad had allowed me to borrow his old bait caster and as we moved out into the water, still covered in a layer of fog, I began whipping casts to any likely looking spots. 'Let's see you put some meat on the table for a change,' Dad had challenged as he handed the rod over. I assured him I'd do my best."

"Well, I didn't get up at five o'clock just to sit and watch my dog pout. I came to fish and I dang well meant to fish! I strained my eyes in the semi-darkness to observe the lucky fisherman who'd just landed that whopper. He was steadily casting and I was trying to catch a glimpse of his lure. It looked like some kind of big floater."

" I snapped open the lid of the cigar box and soon found the nearest thing to it in my collection. It was a large, wooden cigar shaped 'chugger' scooped out in a concave shape at the front to produce a loud 'bloop, bloop, bloop' sound when it was twitched along. It's frog green body was adorned with two sets of the largest treble hooks made by man. The rear end had a small propeller. If these fish wanted noise, I figured this lure was just the ticket. Besides, my friend Pork had one just like it which he claimed to have caught a five pounder on so I figured it must be a good one."

"I tied it on using my best clinch knot and zinged a couple of casts toward the middle of the lake just to get the feel of the rod. 'Not too bad,' I thought as my confidence soared. Then, right behind the boat, a large fish broke the surface. 'Here's my chance,' I thought as I wound up to unleash a mighty cast. I still had about two feet of line dangling from the end of the rod, but I didn't want to hesitate long enough to reel up the slack. I also figured that extra two feet might help get the lure further out in the direction of that big swirl. I reared back and let 'er rip."

"As my arm came forward, the rod was almost wrenched out of my hand. This was followed by the most God-awful wailing sound you ever heard as the bottom set of hooks buried themselves into Butch's hindquarters. Forgetting his fear of water, the terrified dog catapulted himself off the bow of the boat like a torpedo shot from a submarine and began paddling furiously, his only goal being to separate himself from the boat."

"As soon as his nose broke the surface and he was able to get some air into his lungs, a loud mournful 'Aaaaaaroooo! Aaaaaaroooo!' began echoing across the lake. The drag on the reel did its job as line was stripped off, making a loud whining sound. Unfortunately, the line remained intact. I didn't know anything else to do except to try to convince him to return to the boat. 'Butch! Come here boy,' I pleaded to no avail. The drag screaming, the rod bent over and straightened out, we were dragged behind the howling, thrashing mass of black fur. The nearby fisherman, thinking I had hooked a monster bass, began yelling encouragement, 'Play him easy, son. Don't horse him. Give him some line!'"

"All I could do was hang on for the ride, waves lapping against the bow as we gathered speed. Butch had a single mind set and that was to get to shore. I thought of giving him some line but then visualized the chaos which would ensue when he reached shore and tore off through the woods with that lure attached to his hind side. Butch soon began to tire and I gained some line but each time I got close, he found new energy, no doubt by now convinced that I meant to tie him to a stake and torture him. Even as excited as he was, Butch could not keep up his pace forever and began to flounder. I knew I had to do something soon or he might drown."

"The fisherman continued to shout encouragement as I got closer to the frantic animal. We were now only a few feet from shore so I knew the time for action was at hand. Reaching for the large mesh landing net, I held it in one hand while keeping tension on the rod with the other and leaped toward the dog. The boat flipped, throwing me into the water a few feet short of the target. The loud splash urged Butch to greater speed than I thought possible and he began to lengthen his lead. Fortunately for me, I was now in only two feet of water and could run faster than he could swim. I took off after the terrified dog like a sprinter. Butch and I reached shore at the same time. I lunged and grabbed him by the back leg. Big mistake! His teeth as well as the extra sets of hooks began competing for new patches of my skin to puncture."

"But now I had no choice but to hang on 'cause if I let go, he would no doubt tear off again, taking the lure and a good portion of my skin with him. I was finally able to gain enough ground to slither onto shore like a big, mud covered lizard and get a firm grip on him with both arms. I just pulled him to my chest and held on tight. His howling and fierce shaking gradually subsided as he came to the realization that I no longer intended to kill him. It's entirely possible that these few minutes of 'bonding' built up a life long trust between us. I talked softly to him for several minutes and he gradually stopped shaking and began licking my face."

'The nearby fisherman who had observed all this, came over and offered to take us to the emergency room since it was plain to see that each of us had at least two hooks buried to the hilt in our bodies, along with numerous scrapes and cuts. Knowing it would be impossible to ride a bike with one hand while draping a soaked, bedraggled dog over the handlebars, I had no choice but to accept the offer."

"We both survived the ordeal with the worst part of it turning out to be the tetanus shot I had to take. The helpful fisherman turned out to be a friend of my dad's who soon became a steady fishing partner of mine. His ownership of a pickup truck and his own john boat proved to be an unexpected bonus, opening up new horizons on my fishing frontier."

"Butch often accompanied us on these trips, but he and we all agreed that he was much happier on dry ground. On the rare occasions when Butch and I fished from a boat, he discovered that it was more prudent to lie under the front seat than on top of it."

"We enjoyed many years of fishing together, most of which were very pleasant experiences. However, there was one other occasion which was not so pleasant and could have had very serious consequences. But I'm sure you kids have heard enough dog stories, right?"

"No, Gramps," Rod asserted, "We want to hear all your stories." Ellie nodded in agreement.

"Well, there's really only one more so we might as well go ahead and get it out of the way, OK?"

"Yessir," they said in unison. "Let's hear it!"

"We didn't always have a boat, so sometimes I had to fish from shore while Butch would explore. He was a bundle of energy and didn't mind spending hours running around in the underbrush chasing birds, chipmunks and squirrels. On this particular occasion, I had gotten permission from a neighbor who owned a dairy to fish in the pond he used for watering his cows. So I was edging along a wooded shoreline, trying to make as little noise as possible so as not to spook the fish, when I heard some cows begin to moo. This did not concern me as I knew it was customary for cows to come to the pond to drink soon after their morning milking. However, the sound became much more frequent and much louder to boot. There seemed to be some urgency to it as well although I could not figure what cows would have to be urgent about. So I ignored it and continued fishing. All of a sudden, I heard a tremendous crashing sound directly behind me. It sounded like trees were falling. I tuned to look just as a terrified cocker spaniel emerged from the brush headed directly for me. He leaped into my arms, knocking me backwards into the water, which was surprisingly deep at this point. I had just got my feet under me and was standing up when the entire herd of cows came crashing down the embankment and into the water all around me. I couldn't believe my eyes but it was obvious they were chasing Butch. I don't know to this day what he did to irritate them but it must have been something serious because they meant to exact some revenge."

"So there I was in water up to my chest with a terrified dog in my arms, surrounded by thirty or forty angry cows. One or two were blocking my way to shore and showed no inclination to move. The others seemed to be closing in for the kill. Needless to say, I was beginning to get scared. As I pondered a way out of this predicament, it occurred to me that dogs are excellent swimmers and I could swim pretty well, too. So I put Butch in the water and began a slow 'dog paddle' toward the shallow end of the pond with Butch right behind. He wasn't about to let me out of sight. It only took a few minutes and we were clear. Luckily, the cows seemed content with their location and did not follow. The only casualty of this encounter was a busted fishing rod which one of the cows had stepped on. I figured that was a small price to pay for my life."

"Gee Gramps," Ellie exclaimed, "It's hard to believe you came so close to being severely injured or even killed! I don't know what we'd have done without you!"

"Well, Ellie, if I had been killed, you wouldn't even be here."

"Gosh, I guess that's true," she admitted. "I'm sure glad you knew how to swim.

"Me, too, Ellie," the old man replied. "Me, too."

Chapter 8
The Crippled Crane

Gramps motioned silently for Rod and Ellie to stop and be quiet. They were slowly creeping along the edge of the river in search of fresh water clams. Gramma had a recipe for clam soup that would make you forget all about shrimp and lobster. Gramps had mentioned that morning that it had been a while since she made any and she had quickly reminded him of his numerous promises to furnish the key ingredient. After a few muttered comments about being too old to be digging around in the mud, he had relented and promised to make a quick survey of the river bank.

The kids were not about to be left behind. Gramma was always finding something that needed doing like shelling peas or sweeping the yard, so they were always looking for a way to get out of the house. They had set out shortly after breakfast and after only a couple of hours, already had more than enough clams for a large pot of soup. Gramps knew all the little sand bars and sheltered nooks and inlets where clams liked to gather so their task had not been that difficult. He had spied a snowy egret stalking the shallows a few yards ahead, hence his motion for silence. The egret was so intent upon stalking his prospective prey, he had not yet noticed the intruders.

"Let's watch for a spell," Gramps whispered.

One of his favorite activities was observing the nature at work. He would sit for hours watching a spider spinning an intricate web or a sparrow gathering twigs and grass for its nest. In ultra-slow motion, the egret lowered its upraised foot and just as slowly raised the other, the actions taking place at a pace which would making grass seem to grow at breakneck speed. The egret's eyes never lost sight of his selected quarry, the identity of which was yet unknown. Inch by inch the bird seemed to be moving without being in motion. The gap narrowing sufficiently, he made a quick stab with his long, pointed beak which emerged with a squirming young bullfrog neatly impaled. With a quick flip of the bird's narrow head, the frog disappeared down his throat.

"Man, he's quick," Gramps exclaimed. "Did you young'uns see that? Looked like the frog jumped onto that beak without it ever moving. A man with reflexes that quick couldn't be beat at anything!"

The satisfied bird lifted off as gracefully as a ballerina and glided into a shady nook to escape the mid-day sun. "Come on you kids. Let's follow the lead of that clever bird and find us a shady spot for a spell." They climbed a small knoll and settled down under an oak tree sheltering a flat, grassy spot. "How do ya'll like this spot?" he asked.

"Gramps it's a fine spot. Just right for spreading out our picnic lunch." Ellie had a real appreciation for natural beauty.

Leaning a little more to the practical view, Rod chimed in, "Yeah, and I'll bet there's some whoppers in the deep cut under this bank. Sure wish we had brought our fishing rods."

"Well, we just might be able to overcome that little

detail," Gramps had that familiar twinkle in his eye he always got when he had a secret. "Let's see what we have here."

Making a great show of his search, he reached into the pocket of his overalls, but withdrew an empty hand. "Nothing in there." He looked genuinely surprised. "Let's try another one" he teased.

Quick searches of the other front pocket and then both back pockets still produced nothing. "Now I'd a' swore I put 'em in here before leavin' the house." He remarked.

A look of puzzlement came over his face as he said, "Now, let me think a minute." He

raised his cap and began to scratch his head. As he dropped the cap to his side, a small, metal band aid box fell to the ground. "Well, I guess we'll be in good shape if we get a cut, huh, kids," he said.

Rod grabbed the box and was about to hand it back to Gramps when he noticed a rattling noise produced when he shook the box. He pried the lid open and gaped at the contents.

"Oh, wow, Ellie, look," he shouted. "There's hooks, sinkers, bobbers and line in here. All we gotta do is cut us a couple of limbs and we can make our own poles."

Gramps suggested they look a little deeper in the woods where he thought they might find a cane break. If his memory served him right, this was a spot he had frequented many years ago and he knew that cane breaks usually persevered for decades. "Here, Rod," he said. "Take my knife in case you find anything."

Rod went bounding off in the direction indicated and soon returned with three long, limber cane stalks. Gramps performed some magic with his pocketknife and the poles were soon divested of their limbs and were ready for rigging. The lines and tackle were attached and they were ready for fishing.

A sudden thought struck Ellie. "But Gramps, what about bait?" she inquired.

"I was wondering when that would dawn on you,' Gramps chuckled. 'I been lookin' around and I think I saw a couple of spots that might hold a night crawler or two. That old rotten log over yonder looks good. Let's see."

A few minutes of scratching away dead leaves and rotted debris produced a half dozen

fat, juicy worms. "These oughta' be enough to get us started," he said.

Two of the unlucky creatures were soon impaled upon hooks and dropped into the current. Rod and Ellie held the poles at the ready, expecting immediate action. After five long minutes of waiting, they began looking back over their shoulders at Gramps who was seated at the base of the oak with his eyes closed, appearing to be into one of his famous naps. A few more minutes of inactivity brought more looks of bewilderment from the kids.

Gramps finally spoke, "River fishin' fer cats ain't like bream fishin' in a stocked pond. It's way more relaxin'. You got to give 'em time to find the bait. That gives you more time to set down and work out the kinks in your body. Then, too, it's a good time to do some heavy thinking. I had to set me out a pole and watch it for two hours before I could convince myself that I ought to marry your Grandma. So, just set them poles there for awhile and before you know it Mr. Whiskers'll be along for lunch. When he does, you'll have plenty of time to hook 'im, don't worry."

Rod and Ellie looked at each other, shrugged their

shoulders and laid the poles down.

"Here, use these," Gramps instructed as he tossed each of them a forked stick." Somebody must have left 'em lying under the tree," he explained.

Once the poles were set in their holders, there was nothing to do but wait. Each of them expecting that they would be the first to catch one.

"You know, seein' that egret back there reminded me of an experience I had when I was a young lad, still in high school. You wanta hear about it?" Of course they did. He continued. "It was my senior year and I had a summer job to earn a little cash to help out when I started college in the fall. That summer I had a job at a large paper mill. Officially that was the purpose of the mill, to make paper, but sometimes, you would have thought the men who worked there came only to play jokes on one another. Rubber snakes, hand buzzers, whoopee cushions and exploding cigars were standard fare. But every once in a while, someone would get a little more creative. You had to be constantly on alert because anyone telling you anything could be setting you up for the butt of some joke. It had gotten to the point where playing pranks was a major competition among the workers. A 'good one' would be talked about for weeks."

"The favorite time for pranks was during the midnight shift. Since the mill ran 24 hours a day, a crew had to be kept on site at all times, including all night. During the midnight shift, though, there was not much to do unless some emergency repair was needed. Also, the 'big bosses' were seldom present so the men had some time to kill. This was the time when the men could get real creative and, believe me, they came up with some doozies."

"One of the funniest of these involved a crane with a broken wing and a dark bathroom located in an isolated section of the mill. There were many bathrooms scattered throughout the mill, but this particular one had no lights, the bulb having burned out and not been promptly replaced. Whoever used the facility, either had to leave the door cracked so they could see or sit in the dark while they did their business."

"One of the leading jokesters was Smitty, who had found the young, injured crane that afternoon wandering around helplessly in the wood yard. Feeling sorry for the creature, he had put it in a cardboard box, intending to take it home with him for doctoring the next day. In the meantime, after observing several different men enter the darkened bathroom, leaving the door cracked and then exiting, he had a sudden brainstorm."

"He retrieved the box with the crane in it, enlisted two of his co-workers to share the joke and set up a silent vigil, waiting for a victim to present himself. This did not take long as Sam, a huge, overweight black man soon appeared."

"Sam was very regular in his bathroom habits, appearing almost every evening right after dinner and taking a lengthy 'sit-down' while reading the days' newspaper. Sam arrived right on time, dropping his overalls around his knees, and taking a seat, leaving the door cracked so the outside light would enable him to read the newspaper which he had spread out across his knees. Smitty figured this was the opportunity he had been waiting for."

"He quietly removed the crane from the box and set it just inside the open door, slammed it shut and waited. The first sound he heard was a muffled flapping sound as the crane searched for an exit."

"This was quickly followed by Sam's deep voice, 'Hey, you out dare, open de do'. It dark in heah. Good Gawd-amighty! What is you?' Oh Jesus, git 'im off me! Git me outta here!'"

"When the door had slammed shut, the bathroom was immersed in total darkness. The crane became disoriented and began running around, flapping wildly, still trying to find an exit. His instinct being to take flight, he had jumped onto the highest point he could find, in this case, Sam's lap. He tried climbing higher, flapping his wings around Sam's head, his feet digging into Sam's exposed privates, searching for a solid grip."

"Sam was yelling at the top of his lungs for help but soon resolved that none was coming. His only thought now was to get his pants up and rid himself of the devil tormenting him. He accomplished only one half of his goal. He yanked his pants up … with the crane still inside!"

"The door flew open and Sam came out, bellowing like a wounded bull. 'Oh sweet Jesus,' he cried, "What 'dis thang done got in mah pants?'"

"After two steps, Sam's overalls fell down again around his knees and he dropped to hands and knees and began crawling. The terrified bird was still trapped beneath Sam and the ground, still trying his best to escape this mad man, steadily flapping his wings and pecking Sam's face whenever the opportunity presented itself."

"Sam began rolling around on the ground, thrashing like a beached whale, finally disengaging himself from the crane, who immediately sought the safety of the darkened room."

"Sam's eyes, which had been tightly closed for protection during his ordeal, now opened slowly and he discovered that he had an audience. His eyes fixed on Smitty, who, incredibly, was now straight faced."

"'What's the matter, Sam, you havin' a seizure or something?' he asked. 'Lawdy, no, Smitty.' But don't dare go in de toilet. Somethin' in there just beat the hell outta' me!'"

"Smitty could restrain himself no longer, he and his friends breaking out into huge guffaws. Gaining sufficient control to function again, Smitty thought he best show Sam the source of his discomfort. Stepping into the darkened bathroom, he picked up the frightened bird, who had hidden himself in a corner where a small pile of coal was stored."

"The bird was now blackened over most of his body. 'Look here, Sam', you've done scared this bird so bad, you've turned him black'".

"Sam didn't say anything. He simply turned and stalked away, some swearing there was steam coming out his ears. It was a good three month before he even spoke to Smitty again. From then on, he made certain that any bathroom he frequented was well lighted, but he also took along a flashlight, just in case."

Gramps suddenly sat up straight, "Rod, I do believe your pole is about to be drug into the river," He shouted.

"Oh, my gosh," Rod yelped as he leaped for the end of the cane pole which was about to disappear over the bank. His fingers closed on it at the last second and he reared back, a steady, throbbing resistance letting him know he had a solid hook-up. He scrambled to his feet and tried to lift the heavy fish from the water. A deep bend in the pole was all he got for his efforts.

“Easy, son, easy now,” Gramps cautioned. “Don’t try to horse him in. Play him a little first. Looks like a real good ‘un. You can’t just snatch those kind out!”

Rod kept steady pressure on as the fish bored deep, looking for sanctuary in the river channel. Rod managed to turn him just when it looked like the strain would be too much for the limber pole. Ellie was cheering him on as she got more and more excited. She was jumping up and down, screeching out encouragement to her brother.”

The fight became a team effort with Rod the player, Gramps the coach and Ellie the cheerleader. Rod became encouraged as the runs became shorter and the pulsations running up through the pole became slower.

“You’re getting’ there, son,” Gramps continued his quiet words of advice. “but don’t count him just yet. Big cats always give one final lunge before they give up. Be ready for ‘im.”

“I will, Gramps. I’m ready.”

Rod slowly worked the big fish toward the bank, keeping the tip high to try to prevent any more deep runs. They saw a dark shape materialize, then a huge whiskered mouth and two beady little eyes. The fish’s head began to thrash from side to side as it neared exhaustion. It’s every effort to turn back toward the channel was countered by Rod’s deft handling of the pole, as he kept just enough pressure on to turn his head but not enough to break the pole or line. After several minutes of this action, the fish turned and swam toward the bank.

“We’ve got ‘im! We’ve got ‘im,” Ellie squealed at the same moment the fish brushed against an unseen stickup just below the surface.

Instinctively, he turned in that direction and found new

energy for one last lunge. Rod gave line to ease the tension. That tiny bit of slack was all the fish needed.

The throbbing sensation on Rod's line was replaced by a solid, unyielding pressure as the line wrapped around an unseen log. Now the fish had a solid resistance to work against and he used it to full advantage. A loud 'crack' much like a rifle shot announced the bad news to the group. The battle was lost!

They caught a brief glimpse of the giant head as it seemed to grin at them before sinking from sight. Gramps caught Rod and kept him from falling flat on his back. A sick, empty feeling filled the momentary silence as the realization hit them.

Tears welled up in Rod's eyes. "I lost him, Gramps, I lost him. Why'd he have to get around that dern log?"

"Well, son, I reckon he didn't get that big without learning a trick or two. Sometimes, you can do everything right and still lose. I've sure lost my share. Don't you know the big one always gets away? That's where all those sad fishing tales come from. That's just the nature of fishin'. Sometimes you get them, sometimes they get you. This time, he just was a bit luckier than you. Next time, you might be cookin' him up for supper. What challenge would it be if you succeeded every time? The sour taste of losin' is what makes the taste of winnin' so sweet."

"Yessir, I know what you mean, but it still makes you sick." With that, he went stalking over to the tree and sat down with his chin in his hands. Gramps paid him no attention, but instead turned his attention to baiting Ellie's hook with a fresh worm and re-rigging Rod's pole.

A few minutes later, Ellie squealed, drawing Rod out of his sulky mood as he saw the huge bend in her pole.

He involuntarily bounded to his feet and ran over to Ellie's side, offering encouragement.

"Calm down, Ellie. Play him slow and easy. That's the way. Keep him away from that snag."

In a very short time, Ellie proudly lifted the two pounder over the bank and onto the carpet of grass. "Well, he ain't too bad, considering you learned how from me," Rod assured her. Not about to concede anything, she retorted, "At least I caught mine. Yours is still swimming in the river!"

"Not for long, " Rod assured her as he grabbed his pole and began looking for a fresh worm.

Gramps just smiled. "No need to worry about those two," he thought. "They're not quitters."

Feeling a gentle tug, his thoughts were soon directed toward the pressing issue on his own line.

Chapter 9
Southern Boys in Deep Snow

"I ever tell you kids about mine and Weed's snow skiin' adventure?" Gramps asked Rod and Ellie, who had each just devoured a huge slice of watermelon. Ellie looked up with a stream of red juice running down her chin, a seed stuck on her cheek.

"No, sir. I don't believe you ever did," she grinned.

"Lord, just look at the mess ya'll have made. All I can say is don't get it all over your clothes. Your momma'll have my hide."

"Don't worry, we'll clean up real good," Rod assured the old man.

"Sure you will," he said sarcastically. "'Bout like ya'll did when your pups messed up the porch. Thought we'd never get rid of that smell!"

"Aw, Gramps, we've learned our lesson.: Ellie's big brown eyes opened wide and her lashes fluttered.

Gramps looked embarrassed. "Well," he said. "Just see that you do. I don't intend to argue with your momma any more about ya'll's manners.

Both sides knowing the limits to which the other could be pushed, these little give and take episodes had never deteriorated into full-fledged disagreements.

"What about the ski trip?" Rod persisted. The old man's memory was instantly revived. He had stored the memory of that trip for fifty years now and had only retold it a few hundred times at various family gatherings, but never to the kids, who had usually been outside playing at the time. The family had lately seemed to tire of his tales, having heard them so often. The kids, on the other hand, had just reached the age at which they realized that grownups had actually once been children and were curious about their past lives. They were willing to indulge him any time he was willing to tell a story. They hung on his every word, finding in his stories a way to share a part of his life they'd never known and could never know about otherwise. Gramps had watched a TV show involving skiing the night before which had jogged his memory.

"What happened was that two ignorant teenage fools learned to slide down a mountain at Mach I speeds and lived to tell the tale. Me and my buddy Weed Wilkins was invited by your cousin Buck to visit him at his ranch in Colorado. Not having ever set foot outside Georgia before, we were rearing to go. We had a couple of weeks off for Christmas and our parents had miraculously agreed to allow us to ride a bus to Colorado. We couldn't believe they actually let us go. I really think they just wanted some relief from our constant misadventures at home.

"Anyway, we made the arrangements and caught a Greyhound bus as quickly as we could before they changed their minds. We would have only a week for the trip, four days of which we would spend in the bus. That's probably why I've never taken another bus trip in my life. That left us three days to ski, which, we later found out was plenty, believe me."

"We got on the bus in Macon as excited as any two boys could be. We were glued to the windows, not wanting to miss anything. After two hours, we were still in Georgia and began to realize that the scenery had not changed a bit. After four hours, we were well into Alabama, but the scenery still had not changed. Our enthusiasm really began to wane after eight hours and a bellyful of Mississippi and Louisiana whose roads must have been designed by sadists. We seldom hit a smooth spot, making sleep impossible."

"But, since there was nothing else to do, we tried our best to grab a few winks. We must have had a little success because we woke up in Texas. 'Almost there,' we thought."

"Six hours later we were still in Texas! But at least the scenery had changed. Somewhere during the night, we had run out of pine trees. Now we saw plenty of flat, wide open spaces with what little roadside growth there was resembling bushes more than trees. Eventually, even the bushes gave way to long stretches of grassland with nary a tree in sight. I guess we expected to see cowboys riding around everywhere on horses rounding up the cattle and having gun fights in the streets. We were mighty disappointed to see that the people in the few towns we passed through drove cars just like ours, lived in houses much like ours and talked pretty much like us. The boredom which overtook us was like a thick fog from which we could not escape."

"We had completely run out of conversation and really were beginning to get on each other's nerves, arguing about whose turn it was to sit by the window, when we were going to eat, sleep or go to the bathroom. We even had an argument when Weed killed a fly which had lit on my arm. For some reason, I decided that the fly deserved living as much as the rest of us. Of course it wasn't just us who were irritable. The other passengers were just as ready to get off this bus as we were."

"One older man said he had been only a boy when the trip started. A woman with three children said she only had two when she boarded. The bus driver retired and another took his place in New Mexico. You get the idea. The only thing that ever took longer than this trip was the time between Christmases between the ages of three and twelve."

"Buck was supposed to meet us at the station when we finally rolled into Colorado Springs, but he was delayed so we had some time to kill while we waited for his arrival. We had by this time begrudgingly rekindled our friendship. We had little choice as we certainly knew no one at the bus station. Well, kids, I want to tell you, things are a little bit different in Colorado. To a couple of country boys from Georgia, they were a lot different"

"The first thing we noticed was the funny way they talked. We wanted to try our luck on the pinball machines but we didn't have any change. So Weed sauntered over to the counter and addressed the bored looking woman reading a magazine there."

"'Scuse me ma'am,' he began, 'You reckon you could gimme change for this dollah? We wanta play the pinball machine and ain't got no quarters!'"

"Her mouth dropped open and she stared at Weed for a minute before she spoke. When she did, it was in a high pitched nasal tone, pronouncing each word very precisely, 'I beg your pardon, young man?' She had a big question mark on her face like she hadn't heard him although he had spoken quite loudly."

"With a sheepish grin, Weed responded, 'Aw, that's awright ma'am. I didn't even hear you.' He thought she must have belched or something."

"'What do you mean?' she gasped. A red flush slowly creeping over her face."

"'Well,' Weed continued, 'Ain't nobody knows but you 'n me and I sho' don't intend to embarrass a lady by callin' attention to her indiscretions. 'Sides, it happens to all of us at one time or another.'"

"Her response was immediate and indignant, 'I assure you, you uncouth creature, I have no reason for embarrassment!' Judging from her rosy cheeks, however, she was already plenty embarrassed."

"'I just meant it's OK with me if you burp out load any time you want to.' The more Weed tried to appease her, the deeper the hole he was digging."

"Luckily, the woman's co-worker, a pretty young girl, came to the rescue. She recognized that the boys were way out of their element and needed some help."

"'Where are you guys from?' she offered. 'Maude, would you get a load of that accent!'"

"Weed began to enjoy being the center of attention and offered his response in an even more exaggerated drawl, 'We from Georgia,' he said, Georgia sounding like Jawja. 'we done heard 'bout all ya'lls snow out heah and decided to try our hand at snow skiin'"

"Both womens' faces cracked into wide grins at that. 'Would you listen to that!' the older one was loosening up a bit now. 'Say something else, honey chile, Puhleeease.'"

"Rather than being offended as he should have been, Weed was eating it up. 'Sho' 'nuff

Dahlin'. Enny thang yo' little ole heart desires.' It was getting sickening. I finally moved in and called a halt to this scene, reminding Weed that we needed to get to playing before someone else got our machine."

"'Oh, ya'll don't hafta leave right now do you?' the cute young one asked. She, too was getting some fun in at our expense. Weed was too enamoured with her to notice that his leg was getting pulled. As he took a step beck in their direction, I had no choice but to give him a shot in the ribs. 'Hey, Skid, What's your problem?' he muttered. I told him he was making a complete fool of himself and everyone was laughing at us. A quick glance around the room confirmed that fact. 'Oh,' was all he could come up with."

"'Here's ya'll's quawters. Ya'll come back now, you heah!' Maude offered as we grabbed our money and tried to look as inconspicuous as possible. We played the machines without ever glancing at the faces staring in our direction.

"Thirty minutes later, our few quarters were exhausted and we had no choice but to turn away and begin our embarrassing walk out through the crowd. Buck chose this moment to make his appearance. 'Hey, you boys ain't been causin' any trouble, have you?' he greeted us each with a giant bear hug. Ten years older than us, he was now a grown man and knew the score immediately."

"Maude came over all innocent like and addressed our cousin, 'Why Buck, I sure didn't know these little goobers was your friends! I'm afraid we've been down right rude. Please let us make it up to them. Ya'll have a soda on the house!'"

"'All right, Maude, since most of my pay check ends up here every week, I figure you owe me one, anyway.' Maude turned to the young lady. 'Susie, how about getting our guests a couple of sodas. OK boys, what's your pleasure?'"

“Not being familiar with a variety of soft drinks, we assured her that ‘Co Cola’ would be fine.”

“’Don’t you just love it?’ Maude beamed. ‘Co Cola’ it is.’ She wanted to extend this party, but we begged off, explaining that we had big plans for the slopes tomorrow.”

“’Well, you be sure and come by and tell us all about it, OK.’

“’You bet’”, we said as we quickly headed for the door.

“Buck’s father owned a cattle ranch about twenty miles out of town. It was a small operation and he barely made ends meet, but to me and Weed it seemed like paradise. There was a bunk house, a barn for the horses, a smoke house and numerous animals which ranged around the yard free of any restraints. These included chickens, goats, a couple of dogs and a few ducks who kept their distance from the dogs.”

“Two other features made it seem perfect. A small creek meandered through the fenced pasture and except when going to town, everybody rode horses. We didn’t see what else anyone could want.”

“The only drawback was the weather. A constant, biting wind seemed to cut through our bodies. In our world, we were uncomfortable if the temperature dipped below forty degrees. The day we arrived, the temperature was 15 degrees with something called a wind chill factor making it seem like zero! Of course, we weren’t about to let on that a little thing like that bothered us. We traipsed around in our flimsy little wind breakers and worn boots, like this weather was a mild inconvenience at worst. Our excuse for our hasty retreat to the comfort of the roaring open fireplace in the living room was that we wanted to meet the family tonight since we planned to get an early start tomorrow. They seemed to buy it"

"Buck's dad greeted us with another rib cracking bear hug, before turning us over to his wife, Buck's mom, who gave us each a quick peck on the cheek, exclaiming about how much we'd grown in the five years since she had last seen us."

"'You boys just sit and relax for a few more minutes. Supper will be ready, soon,' she piped cheerily. It sure was smelling good, too. And that fire was just the thing. After a few minutes, we shucked out of our jackets and cold boots to better enjoy its bone warming heat."

"The supper which followed was maybe the best I'd ever had at the time and maybe ever since, too. Of course Gamma's being the exception! There were pork chops so tender they slid off the bone and required only the minimum of chewing. There were candied yams so sweet they should have been dessert. There were blackeyed peas so fresh they smelled like the garden in the early morning hours before the sun rose. There were fresh beets, pickled peaches and deviled eggs. There were biscuits still so hot from the oven that butter melted immediately on contact. There was a choice of freshly brewed lemonade or ice cold milk. There was no tea, though, folks in this part of the country not having discovered its particular pleasures. Everyone ate his fill and comments like, 'I'm stuffed' and 'I couldn't eat another bite' came from every corner of the trestle table. Buck's mother would have none of it. 'Glad you boys liked it, because that was just a warm up,' she announced.

"With that she retired to the kitchen where we could hear her clanging a few pots and pans in preparation of her specialty. She quickly returned with a large square baking pan which she held at each end with oven mitts. 'Feast your eyes on this!' she fairly radiated as she set the pan down. She flew back to the kitchen and returned with a stack of bowls which she dealt out like playing cards."

"She began doling out huge helpings of her homemade blackberry cobbler with a spoon the size of a small shovel. When every bowl was full, she used a slightly smaller spoon to dip huge dollops of whipped cream into every one."

"Full or not, we each managed to clean the bowls completely. 'Here, just have a little more,' Buck's mom insisted. I wanted to please her, but could not force down another bite without fear of it all coming back up, so I suggested she save some for our return from the slopes tomorrow. Nodding heads around the table supported me."

"She reluctantly agreed and began clearing the table. This was the cue for the men to retire to the living room for a little light conversation before bedtime. At ten o'clock, Buck's dad announced 'Lights out' and we were herded upstairs to our loft bedroom. I never remember being so worn out or having a more sound sleep."

"The next memory I have is of Buck shaking me awake at 6:00AM. It was still dark outside and I could hear the wind howling. It promised to be another cold one."

"'Hey, Skid, you 'n Weed need to roll out. There's been a change in plans.' A cold feeling suddenly engulfed me."

"'A change in plans?' I spluttered. 'You ain't about to tell me our skiing's cancelled, are you?'"

"'Oh no," he said. 'Nothing that drastic. But we did have some of the cows get out last night and me and my dad have gotta' go round 'em up and fix the hole in the fence. My mom's gonna take you boys over to Broadmoor. Don't look like I'll be able to join you today. You'll find two pairs of skis and ski bibs in the front closet. Ya'll just help yourself. Have fun but be careful. I'll see ya'll tonight. I've got to be going.'"

"With that, he was gone and we were left alone in the darkness of the loft bedroom. Weed sat up rubbing the sleep from his eyes. 'What was that he was saying?' he asked."

"'Oh nothing important. He just said he wasn't going with us today, but his mom was going to drive us. So, I guess we better get on up. I can smell breakfast cooking already.

Man, these folks like to eat!' "

"Fifteen minutes later we were sitting at the breakfast table staring at huge platters of biscuits, bacon and eggs and pancakes. A steaming cup of black coffee sat in front of each of us, flanked by a tall glass of fresh cold milk. We thanked Buck's mom for being so thoughtful."

"'Well, I'm sorry I didn't have time enough to put together a proper breakfast but I promise to do better tomorrow,' she said apologetically."

"I couldn't imagine what she might have added, given enough time. Anyway, we each ate two big helpings of everything and were ready to go."

"'You boys had better get you on some warm clothes. I heard it's going be near ten degrees today. An' as you can hear, the winds kicking up a little, too,' she warned."

"We didn't need to be told twice. We each put on two pairs of jeans and doubled up on socks. We brought out our gloves which we had brought from home and Miss Nell just laughed."

"'I hope you boys don't plan to ski using those flimsy little wool mittens,'" she said. "'Here, let me get you some real gloves.'"

"She went to a closet and emerged with two pairs of thick leather gloves lined with what appeared to be rabbit fur. They sure looked warmer than what we had. She also gave us each a ski mask which was basically a sock with eye holes and a mouth hole. I shudder to think how miserable our day would have been without these additions. After fetching the skis, boots and poles from the closet and loading them into the jeep, we were ready."

"Thirty minutes later, she dropped us in front of the ski lodge, promising to return at four that afternoon. Then she was gone. We were left standing in the parking lot next to a jumbled pile of ski equipment. I felt like we had been deposited into the middle of a foreign country. A foreboding feeling of ill fortune descended upon me and I momentarily wished we had waited until Buck could have come with us. This feeling was immediately pushed aside as Weed's excited yells reached my ears."

"'Would you just look at that view!' he shouted. 'Have you ever seen anything like that? Now that's what I call a mountain.'"

"We had never seen anything larger than the foothills of the north Georgia mountains, which, compared to the majestic peaks surrounding us, were mere mole hills. I had to agree with him. It was pretty impressive."

"Not knowing what else to do, we began to move along a slippery sidewalk toward the entrance to the lodge. There was already a fair crowd gathering and we fell into line like we knew what we were doing. In a few minutes we stood in front of a counter where we purchased our lift tickets. We really didn't know what a lift ticket was but everyone else got them so we figured they must be necessary. They certainly were proud of them tickets, too. That purchase alone almost exhausted our funds."

"With tickets in hand, we shuffled off toward a room which resembled a football locker room with long wooden benches upon which skiers sat, putting on their equipment. We decided to watch others to see what the proper procedure was. The first thing most of them did was pull on their ski bibs, matching gloves, toboggans and glare resistant sunglasses. Since our attire was blue jeans, windbreakers and baseball caps, we only had to pull on the ski bibs, which were really just a pair of waterproof overalls, and wait to see what to do next."

"The next thing they put on were heavy boots which were metal lined and extended further than normal to fit into the bindings of the skis. We overheard several skiers instructing other novices that the bindings should be snug but not too tight which would allow the skis to come off in the event of a fall rather than staying secure and breaking your leg. After donning the boots, we thought we were ready and picked up our skis and headed outside to the snow-covered ground."

"A young man in a bright yellow, skin-tight outfit caught our eye. He seemed to know the ropes so we decided to follow him. He snapped on his skis and poled himself over to a waist high railing which he held onto while he pulled himself over to the entrance to the ski lift loading area. Mr. Yellow Suit, smoothly entered the doorway to the loading shed, waited for the next chair and easily sat down in it and disappeared up the hill. Several others followed him, doing exactly as he did. We did notice several 'beginners' shuffling with great difficulty over toward an area called the 'Bunny Slope' where they seemed to be piling up on one another and having to be untangled by their friends. That didn't seem like the place we wanted to be. Besides, each of us had water-skied many times and we figured that this couldn't be any harder than that."

"We decided to head on up to the 'Intermediate Slope' where people seemed to be having a great time with a minimum of collisions and falls. That seemed to be a more appropriate spot for accomplished athletes like ourselves."

"'That don't look too hard to me,' Weed blurted. He never was one to back off from a challenge. 'Come on. Let's do it!'"

"He slipped on his gloves and ski mask and began to shuffle over toward the rail. He hadn't taken three steps before the skis developed a mind of their own. Apparently they had decided that they had rather not get on the lift. They began to fight him every inch of the way. First the right ski slid away from him at a ninety degree angle while the left one remained stationary. The resultant split evinced a howl of pain followed by a muffled "Umph' as he hit the ground flat on his seat, hands hanging onto the poles which were still stuck into the ground. He first tried to pull the right ski back in toward his body, which appeared to work for a minute, but then the left one shot out away from him causing another split. The image of a marionette being manipulated by a maniacal puppeteer sprang into my mind. The puppeteer seemed to have a sadistic streak"

"Trying to look cool, Weed calmly unsnapped the bindings, picked up his skis and carried them over to the rail. He then hung onto the railing while he snapped the skis back on and nonchalantly pulled himself up the slope. I followed his lead and we were soon in line for our turn."

"Weed wrapped the loops on the poles around his wrists and gently pushed off from the railing. However, instead of gliding forward, as those in front of him had, he began sliding backwards. 'Skid, grab me! Grab me!' he cried as he slid past my position."

"Although the slope was very gentle, he was gaining speed and would soon be out of my range. The only hope I saw was to dive forward and try to hook his ski pole with mine. I soon discovered that you can't dive with skis on. I leaned as far forward as possible but the ski tips prevented me from getting very low. My skis suddenly shot backward, throwing me face first into the snow. By sheer luck, my ski pole was extended just far enough to snag Weed's, snatching him off his feet."

"We now presented a comical scene to those observing our plight. We were both spread eagled, skis crossed behind us, arms extended towards one another with each of our ski poles hooked into the other. As each of us attempted to regain our footing, we only succeeded in pulling the other down again. After a few minutes of flailing around on the ground, we removed our skis again and walked back to the railing, trying to ignore the pitying stares of the other skiers. 'You guys might want to try the Bunny Slope before getting on this lift,' one preppy looking guy advised. 'Yeah, before you kill yourselves,' his buddy agreed.

"'Oh, don't worry about us, we're just a little rusty,' Weed assured them."

"'Yeah, right!' they chorused. "Go see if you can find some WD-40. That can't hurt!'"

"After snapping the skis back on and tightening the bindings a little more just to be safe, we decided it might be a good idea to try to get the feel of it before heading for the lift again."

"We discovered that there is a knack to using the poles. If they are placed too far forward, you are pushed backwards and soon lose control, ending up head over heels in the snow. If they are too far to the rear, the skier will fall backwards as his skis are pushed forward, leaving him suspended in the air, his arms supported by the poles and his feet supported by the rear ends of the skis. Each of us experimented with both methods, eventually discarding both, settling instead for a crablike, sideways shuffle. This method proved to be most stable, even though progress towards the goal was measured in six-inch increments."

"After ten or fifteen minutes of 'practice' we decide to begin our movement towards the railing again. To say progress was slow is an understatement. After an interminable journey during which we were passed by dozens of kids, most of whom were barely out of diapers, the railing was reached once more. With a final sideways fall, we each clung to the railing like drowning men to a piece of driftwood. From there, with the railing serving as our anchor point, it was a simple matter to negotiate the final fifty feet to the loading area. Far too quickly, the skiers behind us were nudging us forward, indicating that it was our turn to board next."

"In the loading area, there is little time to gather your wits. The chairs come by continuously at a constant speed, not slowing down to allow you to climb aboard. The idea is that the skier positions himself in front of the moving chair which then hits the backs of his legs, causing him to sit down and he is quickly swept off his feet and carried away up the slope."

"When our turn came, we crab-crawled into position as quickly as we could, but still barely had time to stand before the chair was upon us. It struck our legs just as planned and we quickly sat down. And I do mean quickly. Our rear ends hit the chair with a loud 'WHOOMP!' initiating a bouncing motion, tossing us about like a couple of rag dolls. If not for the vice-like grips we had on the arm rests, we would no doubt have been thrown out."

"The chair slowly settled down and we began to relax and enjoy the ride. The scenery was gorgeous from 30 feet in the air. The ski slope was a white, snow covered ribbon, flanked on both sides by bushy fir trees, the snowcapped peaks of the Rockies overlooking it all. 'Man, it sure is pretty!' Weed was impressed with the sheer beauty of the place. 'There sure ain't nothing like this back home, is there?' I agreed. 'Yeah, I guess not but they ain't got no swamps here, so I guess it's a fair trade,' I said."

"We were so wrapped up in the scenery that we didn't notice the dismount area coming up. The way that works is that a flat topped mound is built up to within a couple of feet of the chair lift and the skiers are supposed to stand when their skis make contact with the top of the mound. The continuous forward motion of the chair against the back of the legs pushes the skier along until he slides down the front of the mound which slopes off toward the entrance to the ski trail, carrying the skiers out of the way of those behind."

"We had not been paying attention to this procedure and hardly noticed when our skis made contact with the mound. Just as we reached the point at which the slope began falling away, we both realized that we were supposed to dismount here. As our skis left the ground it became apparent that it was too late to dismount in the usual manner. Not wanting to ride all the way around again and be embarrassed again by everyone waiting for an empty chair at the bottom, we decided to jump. After all it was only about four feet."

"By the time we gathered ourselves enough to leave the chair, that four feet had grown to eight feet, then ten. But, once the commitment to jump was made, there was no reversing it so jump we did. Miraculously, we each hit on our skis and began a very rapid descent down the slope, each of us clutching the other for support. This movement soon degenerated into a total tangled mess, consisting of skis, poles, arms and legs. Sliding and rolling down the slope, we hit the huge pool of slush which had accumulated at the bottom at a speed sufficient to shoot a plume of water and ice ten feet into the air."

"The pool had one positive effect, though. It cushioned the blow enough to avoid serious injury. The negative part was that we were now soaked to the bone. As we began untangling ourselves and crawling out of the freezing slush pool, I glanced up and saw a small booth occupied by the ski lift operator. He had quickly fashioned a makeshift sign on which he had inscribed with a magic marker the numerals '9.9'. His grinning face flanked one side of the sign and his other hand showed a 'thumbs up'. He probably hadn't seen a dismount that entertaining in years.

"We finally extricated ourselves from the icy muck and stood once again on dry land. It was by no means level land but it was dry. Being very careful not to let our skis get pointed down slope, we assessed our situation. We were both shivering uncontrollably. When I suggested to Weed that we go back to the lodge and call Buck's mother to bring dry clothes, he acted like I'd suggested he eat cow manure. His face exhibiting an expression best described as sinister, his teeth chattering, he stuttered, 'I d-d-d-n'y c-c-c-ome, fif-fif-teen hundred m-m-m-iles to s-s-s-it at h-h-h-ome! I'm go-go-go-na ski if it k-k-k-k-ills me!' From the looks of him, I thought it might. The lift operator came to our rescue."

"'Hey, you boys come on over here,' he yelled."

"We thought we had probably broken some rule or other and meekly sidestepped over."

"'You fellas take those skis off and come inside. I want to show you something'. Still not convinced he was up to any good, but having few options, we complied. It was the best decision we made that day. What he showed us was a potbellied Franklin stove which was fully fired up and radiating an unbelievable warmth. On the stove was a kettle, which, from the smell of it, contained hot chocolate.'"

"'My names, Ike,' he said. 'Please excuse my little joke with the sign. I couldn't resist. I just thought you might welcome a little relief from the cold. Nothing like a good cup of hot cocoa to warm the old bones. You're welcome to set a spell, have a cup and let those clothes dry off a little.'"

"We couldn't believe our good fortune. It was all we could do to resist hugging that wonderful little heater. 'T-t-t-hanks, M-m-mister.' Weed croaked, 'W-w-w-we could use s-s-s-some.'"

"Ike poured us some cocoa and in a few minutes we

began to feel human again. An hour of that heat and our clothes were dry enough to tolerate and we were ready to try again. Ike advised us to take it easy until we got the 'feel' for it and to come back and see him if we needed warming up again. We thanked him and slowly made our way to the edge of the intermediate slope. I bent down to adjust the bindings on my skis and reminded Weed not to make them too tight."

"I discovered I was talking to myself as Weed was no longer within earshot. I scanned the surrounding area and he was nowhere to be seen. My attention was drawn to a skier 100 yards down the slope flying into the air as a blue/brown blur flew past him. Weed was hurtling straight down the slope, arms wind milling, ski poles flailing the air, his speed increasing at an alarming rate. A hideous sound I can only describe as resembling that of a freshly castrated hog, was emanating from his lungs at full volume."

"Taking note of the plate glass window of the lodge looming at the bottom of the slope, protected only by a small wooden fence, I could only hope that something would slow him down. My hopes were fulfilled."

"His feet shot out from under him and he landed flat on his back and seemed to explode. Snow, mixed with ski poles, gloves and skis flew in all directions. Only the fact that he tumbled end over end, rather than rolling, saved his legs from being horribly twisted. As it was, only his head was injured, having been rapped severely by a ski pole as it plummeted back from the orbit into which it had been launched by his momentum."

"As I anxiously waited in vain for some movement from the brown and blue lump lying in the snow, I feared for his life. Then his legs began to twitch slowly. This was followed by several weak attempts at raising his head. Slowly, he drew his knees into his chest and assumed the fetal position. Then he rolled over onto his hands and knees. Realizing that he wasn't dead, he gathered his wits and suddenly let out one of his famous yells, 'Wheeeeaaaah!!! Hot Dog, Skid. Did you see that? Man, I must a been doin' ninety. You seen my skis? I cain't wait to try this sucker again.'"

"After witnessing perhaps the most awesome fall in the history of skiing, my enthusiasm was somewhat less than Weed's. However, I, too, had travelled fifteen hundred miles for this and I wasn't about to pass up the opportunity either. Gathering Weed's scattered equipment, we began in earnest to try and master this sport."

"By lunch time, we had gained a reasonable degree of proficiency and could sometimes make it down the entire run with only three or four falls. Weed must have felt that this made him an expert and now he was ready for new challenges. 'Hey, Skid,' he suddenly suggested. 'You ready to get off this sissy slope and get on up yonder where the men are?'"

"I was somewhat less than enthusiastic. 'Weed, we've hardly learned enough to get down this little slope yet without wipin' out and …' He cut me off in mid protest. 'Aw come on, man. Snow is snow. What difference does a little steeper slope make? Besides, just look at them little kids flyin' down that hill. You ain't gonna let them show you up, are you?'"

" I assured him I was. 'I intend to live to be an old man. You can go kill yourself if you want to, but I'm gonna stay here and practice a bit more.'"

"'Suit yourself, you big wimp,' he teased. He was

trying to shame me into going along, but I was having none of it."

"'Just watch out when I come through,' he continued, 'because I'll be truckin'. Now stand back and learn.!' He stalked off in the direction of the lift and was soon out of sight."

"Then I remembered my promise to his mother that I would look after him on this trip. It was part of my argument to convince her to let him come. She knew he was not afraid to try anything and she needed some assurance that I would at least try to restrain him if he got too near the edge of reasonable behavior. Not wanting to have to explain to her that I had stood by and let him kill himself or someone else, I decided that I better catch him"

"'Hey, Weed,' I shouted. 'Wait up. You ain't gonna have all the fun!' That vague sense of foreboding disaster began to slowly seep into my inner being again."

"In a very short time, we were deposited at the top of the mountain. The view before was awesome but this was beyond description. We could see all the way down into the valley where houses were the size of match boxes and cars seemed to be tiny beetles crawling among them. The town of Colorado Springs looked like my mother's Christmas Village when she set it up each year. For a few long seconds, we just stood there and soaked it in. This was a once in a lifetime experience and we both knew it. Our reverie was broken by the harsh voice of an impatient skier behind who bellowed, 'You boys going to ski or sight see?' as he elbowed by us and quickly disappeared down the slope."

"As we watched him go, we were finally forced to look at the sheer terror-inspiring slope which lay before us. It reminded me of standing on the roof of my house and knowing that if I ever started sliding, I could never stop. We sucked in our collective breaths as we realized what a predicament we had gotten ourselves into. Not only was the slope roughly equal to that of a church steeple, it was covered with huge mounds of hard packed snow they called *moguls*. These were designed to give the skier a challenge and offered the opportunity to do some maneuvering rather than sliding straight down. They looked to me more like an obstacle course designed to break a maximum number of bones."

"I glanced at Weed before he'd had a chance to don his 'game face' and what I saw was not encouraging. His face was white and his eyes were bugged out, his mouth agape. Then, as he glanced my way, an instant transformation occurred, his face changing instantly into the one I was more familiar with. With an air of bravado, he gushed, 'Just look at that hill, would you. Have you ever seen such a sight? Look at that guy flyin.'"

"He was pointing at the yellow suited skier we had followed that morning as he flew past and expertly banked off two moguls and executed a mid-air 'three-sixty' before landing smoothly and continuing his blazing descent. The man was obviously way past pretty good. He looked like Olympic Games material to me but he just inspired Weed more."

"'Hey, Skid, watch this,' he warned as he stepped off the small ledge we were standing on and was gone. I had only thought he was moving fast on the first run that morning on the intermediate slope. Now his speed was approaching that of the average NASCAR racer."

"He headed for the first mogul, poles tucked under his arms, knees slightly bent seemingly in perfect position.

Ten feet short of his goal, he lost his nerve. His form disintegrated into the familiar elbows, knees and skis posture with which I had become familiar and he plowed into the bank face first. Like a rag doll, he bounced into the air, flipped and landed on his skis again, still accelerating. 'HELP…I can't stop!' he warned those unsuspecting souls below. Then he hit the second mogul."

"This time, determined not to lead with his face, he leaned back, letting his ski tips absorb the initial shock. As his skis shot up the slope, the rest of his body, led by his rear end, began bouncing along behind, the back of his head leaving a furrow in the wake. He ricocheted off the mound like a pinball off a bumper, returning to earth again twenty yards downslope and tumbling along in a tangled mass until he abruptly came to rest against the base of a huge fir tree, which dumped a load of fresh snow on top of him."

"All I could see of him was a white lump with a couple of skis protruding. Not wishing to share his fate, I unsnapped my skis and began sliding on my rear end down the slope toward his position. Even without skis, my descent was far more rapid than I'd planned. Also, I could not maneuver and soon saw that my projected path would not take me to Weed's position."

"In order to gain some control, I needed to slow down. This was accomplished by hooking my ski pole around a small sapling as it flashed past. The problem was that my deceleration was anything but gradual, almost yanking my arm out of its socket."

"Nevertheless, my first goal was accomplished. Now I had to figure out how to cross the slope to get to Weed's still unmoving form. I slowly pulled myself up to a sitting position, still desperately hanging onto the tree. This gave me a small degree of security from which to launch my mission. Gathering my knees up under me, I began a slow crawl across the thirty yards of slippery slope between me and Weed. I was so intent on my goal, I failed to notice the red blur of a ten year- old bearing down on me. He struck me square in the side, and we both began to tumble out of control, locked to each other like a pair of sumo wrestlers, grunts, groans and moans pouring forth. Luckily, the kid knew enough to 'spread eagle' his body to stop the tumbling. Even so, we still slid another thirty yards before easing to a stop, now well below Weed's position. 'Sorry, little fella', I didn't see you,' I got out before he lit into me. 'Jeez, you idiot. Where you from anyway? Don't you know better than to go crawling across a ski slope?'"

"Actually, I didn't but I felt it best not to press the point. I nodded in the affirmative and began crawling again. Before I had gone ten feet, I was bowled over again, this encounter knocking the wind out of me and rekindling my dormant temper. 'Man, give me a break, will you. I'm not from around here and I really don't appreciate being knocked around every time I turn around and … Wait a minute, this guy looks familiar,' I thought.

"'Skid, It's me', he shouted."

"Unbelievably, it really was Weed. I couldn't believe he was even alive, much less skiing. His stamina and guts were amazing, the stuff legends are made of."

"He continued, 'I thought I was a goner, but that tree saved me. Get your skis on and lets do 'er again.'"

"'Not on your life. I've had about all the skiing I can handle for one day. I'm still in one piece and I aim to stay that way. I'm going to walk down'"

"And that's what I did. I walked all the way down, caught the lift back up, retrieved my skis and spent the rest of the day in the coffee shop, enjoying the warmth and admiring the scenery. Weed, of course, continued his one-man crusade to set the record for the most bruises ever suffered by one body in one day. I don't know if he succeeded but, if he didn't, I would hate to see the guy who holds it"

"After another good hour of slipping, sliding, tumbling and crashing, Weed finally decided to pack it in and limped into the coffee shop. He was insistent that we make plans to come back the next day. I was noncommittal, saying that we'd have to see what Buck had planned for us."

"The decision was made easy for us when neither of us could get out of bed the next morning. We had pains in places we didn't know we had places. The pain was even worse the next morning. Buck's family didn't miss an opportunity to rub it in."

"'You greenhorns need to toughen up before coming back up here,' they would say, with a little wink to whoever was in earshot"

"We were still thankful for their hospitality and managed to help with a few chores before our departure time arrived. As we bid them goodbye, they made us promise to come back soon and we promised we would. Sadly, we never got the opportunity again. It truly was a 'once in a lifetime experience."

"Could you take us one day, Gramps?" Rod asked.

"Yeah, could you, Gramps? It sure sounds like fun," Ellie chimed in.

"Well," Gramps said. "I'm a little old for that sort of

thing now. You better talk to your dad. Or better yet, it'll only be a few years before you'll be able to make the trip on your own like we did. For now, though, you'll just have to make do with my memories."

Chapter 10
Old John Hicks

Gramps and the kids pulled into the parking lot at the State Bank & Trust early one Friday afternoon. Gramma always sent Gramps to the bank on Friday to get her a "little change" for the week end. She says you never can tell what may come up that requires cash and she never wanted to be completely short. Gramps knew she really meant she was going to town on Saturday and wanted to be prepared for whatever sale may come her way. She never had really taken to writing checks and she surely was not keen on the idea of credit cards. She felt they were too risky.

"If I can get stuff with it, someone else can, too," she was fond of saying.

As usual, the lot was full, Friday being pay day. Nearly everyone in town came to the bank on Friday and he knew that he might as well not get in a hurry. It took about fifteen minutes for him to get his turn.

"Good mornin' Mr. Skidmore!" his favorite teller, Margie called. He always went to her since she knew him well and didn't bother him with producing an ID.

"And who have we here?," she asked as she gushed over the kids. "These cain't be the same children you brought in last year, can they? Why they sure have grown. You been feedin' 'em some of your magic fertilizer? They're even cuter than I remember."

"Yep, this is them, Margie. They're here for their summer visit. 'Gonna be here for a month. I'm sure you'll see them some more before they go back to the city." Gramps was proud to be showing off his grandkids.

"Well I'll sure be lookin' forward to that," Margie said. "Say, do you kids like suckers? I thought so. Who doesn't?" she exclaimed as she produced a bowl of multi-colored suckers. "Ya'll pick out whatever flavor you want. I just love the cherry ones, myself!"

Rob and Ellie took little time, each digging out a cherry flavored pop. "I knew you kids had good taste," Margie winked. "Just like your grandpa. You know, me and your grandma had a thing for old Skid here a long time ago. I could just as easily have been your grandma myself. Now wouldn't that be something?"

"Now, Margie, let's not get too personal, you hear!" Gramps snorted. He was obviously embarrassed, which pleased Margie immensely.

"Well it's true and I always say 'Honesty is the best policy.' Anyway, Skid give us both a fair try, I will say that for him. Your grandma just seemed to have a little better skill in the kitchen. You know, the way to a man's heart is through his stomach, don't you? Anyhow, we did have some good times while it lasted, huh, Skid?"

Gramps' face was now a bright scarlet. "That's enough, Margie. You'll give the kids the idea I was some kind of Romeo".

"Well, so what? They should be proud you were such a popular guy. As I recall, me and Irene wasn't the only ones you were stringin' along were we, Skid? You kids need to dig out his yearbook sometime and read the comments in the margins. You'll see for yourself, believe me!"

The children were all ears now, wanting to hear more but the line was long and a man behind them cleared his throat a little louder than necessary, letting them know it was time for them to move on. Gramps was eager to oblige him. "OK, kids, time to get on to the grocery store," he growled. " Gramma needs some stuff for supper." With that, they reluctantly bid farewell to Margie, who was still grinning wickedly at their grandpa.

"Gramps," Ellie asked, "Can we look at your yearbook when we get home?"

"We'll see. I don't think I even know where that thing is anymore." He pretended to be looking for the car keys as he brushed off the request.

"I'll bet Gramma does!' Rod volunteered. "She always puts stuff up where she can find it later."

"Now, don't you be botherin' your Gramma, you hear," Gramps commanded as he started the car. "She has enough on her mind."

"Sure thing, Gramps," Rod promised while he made a mental note to ask her the first chance he got.

Gramps knew it was time to change the subject. The trip to the bank had triggered some long dormant memories. He had worked for a summer at this same bank when he was a high school senior and had gotten very familiar with many of the local characters. One of his favorites was the proprietor of the local general store, Old John Hicks.

Of course, with him being a teenager and Mr. Hicks being a man in his seventies at the time, he never called him by anything other than Mr. Hicks or Mr. John, as was the custom. Now that he himself was a man in his seventies, he felt justified in calling him Old John Hicks in his recollections about his friend.

Mr. Hicks came into the bank often and usually stopped for a chat with the young Skidmore before returning to the store. They got to be pretty close after a few weeks and Mr. Hicks began to confide in the young man many of his "secrets". He always seemed to have an amusing anecdote to share and the boy was always willing to listen to the old man. It was good that he had the blessings of his boss who was one of Mr. John's oldest and dearest friends. Otherwise, he could have been criticized for "wasting time" with customers. Instead, his boss encouraged the relationship, stating on several occasions, "Anything Mr. John wants, you let him have." As the relationship grew, so did the complexity and length of the stories.

"Did I ever tell you about my days in banking?" Gramps asked innocently.

Although he had, they did not let on and chimed in, "No. Gramps. When were you ever in banking?"

"When I was just a teenager, about to enter the real world, I worked a couple of summers in the bank and got to know one old man real well. Did I ever tell you about Old John Hicks?"

He never had told them about Mr. Hicks, so this immediately drew their interest. "No sir. Who's he?" Ellie asked.

"Why, just one of the wisest men I ever met, is all," he said. "He taught me more about human nature and the value of honesty and kindness than almost all the other people I knew put together. Soon as we get these groceries and take them to your Gramma, I'll have to tell you about him."

An hour later, the groceries had been delivered and the kids and their grandpa had an hour or so to kill while supper was being prepared and took seats in the den, each of them with a tall glass of lemonade to sip on.

"OK, now you can tell us about Old John Hicks," Ellie reminded him.

"Oh, yeah. I promised didn't I?" Gramps conceded.

"Well, Old John Hicks was one of my favorite customers during my banking days. He used to come around to see me and always had a story or two to tell me. One of his favorites was about the very early days of his marriage to his beloved Juliette. Old John was a very wiry man, some might even say skinny, but he said that soon after his marriage, he began to put on weight and his wedding band began to feel a little tight on his finger. He ignored it for a few weeks, but as the steady diet of meat and potatoes did their work, the ring became tighter and tighter."

"He tried several times to get it off his finger for some temporary relief but, try as he might, it would not budge. The last thing he wanted was to tell Juliette because they had each promised they would never remove their rings for any reason. Eventually, the pain became so severe, he knew he had to do something or suffer some permanent damage."

"After one day of particularly excruciating pain, he decided that, whatever the consequences, today, he would have to tell Juliette of his dilemma."

"As he arrived at his home, he found his bride busily preparing supper in the kitchen. Coming up behind her, he gently wrapped his arms around her and turned her to face him. Looking deep into her puzzled eyes, he mustered his sincerest voice and whispered, 'Juliette, darling. I've got something to tell you that I hope you'll understand."

"Why, John, that sounds serious," she said. "What in the world is it?'

Juliette, I know we promised, but I've got to do something about this ring. My fingers have swelled since we got married and now this ring is cutting off my circulation!'"

"Just as sincerely, she gazed back into his eyes and stated: 'Why, John, you silly thing, that's what it's supposed to do!' Old John swears the ring never bothered him again"

"Old John, like many merchants of that day, sold mostly on credit. That is, he let people maintain a running bill with him. They could get groceries and other items as they needed them and then pay him at the end of the month. Trouble was, many of his customers were dirt poor and often could not pay him when the bill came. This sometimes caused him to lose money, even though sales were good. Somehow, though, he managed to keep his own bills paid."

"He came in one day on a Friday, which, for him, like the bank's, was one of his busiest days. He stopped by my desk and sat down as he usually did to pass the time. I asked him, 'Mr. John, who's running the store?'"

"'No one,' he replied."

"'Well,' I asked, 'Aren't you worried about losing business?'"

"'On the contrary,' he replied, 'Business is so good, I couldn't afford to stay open!'"

"Another time, Old John came in and told me about a lady customer he had had earlier that day. Mrs. Hubbard was a regular customer of his and he valued her business, but she was always complaining about one thing or another particularly prices. Having dealt with her as a bank customer, I knew exactly what he was talking about. He said she had come into his store that morning and asked if he had any pork chops. He answered in the affirmative."

"'Well,' she demanded, 'How much are they?'"

"'They're $ 1.39 per pound,' he replied."

"'Why that's ridiculous, Mr. Hicks,' she snorted, 'Mr. Smith only charges $ 1.29 at the Red & White Store.'"

"'Well, in that case, madam,' he patiently asked, 'Why didn't you buy them from Mr. Smith?'"

"'Because, if you must know, Mr. Smith is out of pork chops!'"

"'Well, Mrs. Hubbard,' Old John smiled. 'When I'm out of 'em, I only charge $ 1.19!'"

"Old John couldn't control the twinkle in his eye as he described her haughty and hasty departure."

"He really sounds like a great guy to talk to, Gramps," Ellie said.

"He was," Gramps asserted. "If the world was full of people like Old John, it would be a much better place. That was proven at his funeral a few years later. Almost everyone in town attended. Most of them owed him money and were forever grateful for his kindness to them over the years. I never heard anyone say an unkind thing about Old John Hicks. There were many other funerals in that small town, many for people who were much better off financially than Old John. There never was one which was better attended, nor was there one during which more praise was lavished. I think Old John himself would have been embarrassed over all the 'to do' about him."

"He had never sought accolades during his life and would have thought himself totally undeserving. How wrong he would have been. He is the prime example of my belief that some men obtain their rewards while on earth in the form of praise, riches or power. Real men, like Old John Hicks receive their just rewards in heaven, just as Jesus intended."

"Now, let's go see what Gramma's got cookin'!"

Chapter 11
Pranks

Gramps could tell the moment he saw the expression on Rod's face that something had upset him. He had obviously been crying but was trying his best to conceal that fact. He let the screen door slam behind as he started to bound up the stairs to his room, taking the steps two at a time. Gramps wisely gave him a few minutes to compose himself and then quietly made his way up the stairs, standing at Rod's door listening to his sobs. He gently tapped on the door and heard Rod respond, "Just a minute, OK?"

"Sure, son," Gramps conceded. "I can wait, but I've got something to tell you that you may want to know." A second before, Rod had had no interest in anything but himself and his hurt feelings, but now his curiosity was piqued and he just had to know what Gramps wanted to tell him. He quickly wiped his face, took a few deep breaths and slowly opened the door.

"Mind some company, young man?"

"Sure, Gramps," Rod whispered. "You know I've always got time to listen to you."

"Well, in this case I think I may need to listen to you first. What's ailin' you son?"

"Oh, Gramps, it's nothin' you'd be interested in. Just some of the guys acting the fool made me mad."

"Well, tell me about it anyway. I've lived a good long

while and learned a few things along the way. Maybe I can help. But even if I can't, there's no harm in sharing. You know, a load shared is only half as heavy!"

Rod figured there was no harm in telling the old man. He might even get a good laugh, much as his buddies had. "Gramps, you know I'm in the Boy Scout troop, right? Well, tonight Mr. Winston played a trick which embarrassed me pretty good. Everyone was in on it and I've caught grief ever since."

"Rod, you know I was in the 'Scouts myself and we were always pulling one prank or another. As long as no one was injured, I didn't see the harm. In fact, I pulled some doozies myself. You weren't hurt, were you?"

"No, sir, not physically anyway. Just totally embarrassed. I can't face those guys after being so stupid."

"Oh, it can't have been that bad. Go ahead and let's hear it. I see the front of your jeans are wet. They didn't pull the old 'Hand in the pan of warm water' trick did they?"

"No, how does that work?"

"Well, usually it's pulled on a camping trip where the first guy to fall asleep has his hand placed in a pan of warm water. For some reason, this causes him to wet himself. You talk about embarrassing. That happened to me on my first camping trip over 50 years ago and some of the culprits still get a giggle out of remembering it."

"No, Gramps, that's not what happened. But I almost wished it had. At least in that case, I would have had no control or knowledge of the situation. What happened was this:

Mr. Winston announced that he wanted to see who had the best coordination by seeing who, while blindfolded, could successfully drop a quarter off their chin into a funnel which was stuck into their pants at the belt line. Ronnie Braxton tried it first and got it on the third try. Jimmy Peeler got it on the fourth try. Every boy tried before me and most of them got it in less than three tries. Finally, it was my turn. Mr. Winston placed the blindfold across my eyes and jammed the funnel into my pants. Then he told me to hold my head back and placed the quarter on my chin. As I was about to drop the quarter, he poured a cup of cold water into the funnel. He and the guys then started laughing at me. All I could hear was the guys laughing and then they started chanting, 'Roddie wet his pants! Roddie wet his pants!' Gramps, I snatched the blindfold off and ran from the room and I ain't ever going back!"

Gramps could hardly hold his own laughter. It was one of the best pranks he'd heard of and no one was really hurt, so he knew he had to make Rod see that such shenanigans were a natural part of a boy's life experience and ultimately would help him learn to cope with much more serious or embarrassing situations which were sure to come. But at the moment, he did not want to add to Rod's discomfort, so he decided to 'one up' him.

"Rod, I know how much it hurts inside to be the butt of jokes, but it's something we all have to endure at one time or another. The trick is to not let them know how much it bothered you or you'll become their favorite target. If you just laugh it off, chances are next time they'll pick on someone else. They're like a pack of wolves, you know. They always go for the weak or unsuspecting. If you prove you can take it, they'll be less likely to dish it out. Or, you may want to give them a taste of their own medicine!"

"Oh, I'd love to do that! But how? I don't know any tricks to play on them, " Rod whined.

"Oh, but I do, boy. I do!"

"And you'd be willing to help me get revenge?"

"Revenge is such a harsh word. Why don't we say we'll show them that two can play the same game."

"Well, whatever you want to call it, I'm ready!"

"OK. When is your next camping trip?"

"It's in two weeks. Is that enough time?"

"Oh, that's perfect. Just perfect." Gramps eyes glowed with the thought of his plan. He only hoped Rod had the ability to pull it off. He felt confident he did. It was sure worth a try, anyway.

During the two weeks before the camping trip, Gramps explained the plan to Rod so many times, Rod was getting tired of hearing about it. But Gramps insisted that, in order to work, the prank had to be carefully planned and then acted out with a convincing performance. He would have to enlist at least one of the other Scouts and Rod chose his best buddy, Franklin Motes. Franklin was a little older and had been with the troop long enough to gain the respect and trust of all its members. He quickly became a willing accomplice after being sworn to secrecy.

The next order of business was choosing the victim. It didn't take Rod long to settle on Ronnie Braxton. He was the self-proclaimed leader due to his size and the fact that his father owned more land in the county than any other ten men combined. He had developed a superiority complex and was always lording it over on the other guys about what expensive clothes he wore or at what well-known resort his family vacationed. He was something of a braggart although he had never really excelled at anything himself. He was long overdue for a lesson in humility.

The day of the camping trip finally arrived and Gramps went over the plan one more time before Rod and the other boys were loaded onto the bus, emphasizing again the need for complete sincerity and acting ability for the plan to work. After a two-hour trip deep into the woods, the bus finally stopped at a primitive campground and the boys soon had their tents set up and were given an hour of free time before supper.

Rod knew this would be a good opportunity to put the plan into operation. He nodded at Franklin and initiated the plan by loudly asking, "Have any of ya'll ever seen a horse hair rope?"

No one seemed very interested at first but he continued, "It's the strongest rope known to exist. My grandpa says they were real common when he was a kid but no one makes 'em any more. He let me bring one of his on the trip in case we have any heavy loads to lift. He says he's never seen one broken, no matter how much weight is put on it. I've seen him myself use it to hoist motors out of cars or to pull stuck tractors out of the mud. He says that even one strand across a man's nose will keep him from raising his head off the ground."

"Aw go on, Roddie. You 'spect us to believe that hogwash?" It was Ronnie Braxton right on cue. "Ain't no single strand of hair that strong."

"Well, my grandpa says it is and I believe him," Rod retorted.

"Well I gotta see it to believe it." Ronnie had thrown down the gauntlet, just as Gramps had predicted he would.

"OK. You want to see it proven, I'll show you.

Franklin, you're the biggest boy here. If it will hold you down, it'll hold anyone down. You want to try it?" Rod had carefully extracted a single strand of horse hair about a foot long from the rope and was holding it up for all to see.

"I don't know, Rod. One strand seems pretty flimsy to me," Franklin was playing his part perfectly.

"Well, in that case, it'll be easy to prove me wrong, won't it?" Rod was getting into the act pretty well himself now.

"Ok, I guess you won't be happy 'till somebody shows you how dumb you are again. Might as well be me. What do I need to do?"

"Here's the deal. Gramps says it's really a trick your mind plays on you. If you can't see the size of something, it's easy to believe it is bigger or stronger than it really is. So, I have to blindfold you and then you lie flat on your back. I'll hold the hair across your nose and you won't be able to raise your head and break it."

Without warning, Ronnie stepped forward and snatched the hair from Rod's hand and snapped it in two as easily as if it were spaghetti. "Yeah, Roddie, we see how strong it is. What a load of malarkey!"

"That's just the point, Ronnie, you can break it if you can see it but not if you can't. Let's see if Franklin can do it blindfolded. Then we'll see who's right." Rod had extracted another strand of hair and was waving it around as he had before.

Franklin spoke up, "Come on, Ronnie, I want to try it. Rod seems determined to prove again how gullible he is."

With that, Rod quickly fashioned a blindfold from his Scout bandanna and tied it across Franklin's eyes.

Franklin lowered his body to the ground and rolled onto his back. "OK, Rod, let's see what you got."

Rod stood at Franklin's head and stretched the horse hair taut between his two fists and lowered it slowly until it rested across Franklin's nose. "OK, Franklin, try to raise up."

Franklin made a great show of attempting to raise his head, being careful not to exert enough pressure to actually break the hair. He appeared to be straining with all his might with no success. After a few moments, Rod asked, "Give up?"

"I can't believe it. I couldn't budge it, guys." Franklin was very convincing.

"Well, well Ronnie. I told you didn't I?" Rod stood up triumphantly.

"Not so fast, nerd," Ronnie taunted. "Seein' ain't always believin' and I still don't believe you. It has to be some kind of trick."

"Well, you're welcome to try it yourself," Rod said. "'Course, if Franklin can't do it, I doubt if you could either." Ronnie knew a dare when he heard one and he was not one to back down.

"Alright, then. I still think it's ridiculous and I'll prove it. Gimme that blindfold."

Rod could hardly contain his glee, but managed to keep a straight face as he tied the blindfold around Ronnie's eyes. Ronnie quickly dropped to the ground and grumbled, "Let's get this over with."

Rod handed the horsehair to Franklin who quickly knelt at Ronnie's head and lowered the hair to Ronnie's nose. At the same time, Rod dropped his pants and as Franklin gave the "Go" signal for Ronnie to raise his head, Rod stepped across Ronnie's chest and lowered his buttocks to within a few inches of Ronnie's face. Ronnie's head immediately broke the hair and his nose was momentarily jammed between Rod's bare buttocks. The boys surrounding Ronnie howled with glee. Ronnie's embarrassment was only exceeded by his anger.

Rod rolled out of the way as Ronnie snatched off the blindfold and started for him with nothing in mind other than making Rod pay dearly for his brief triumph. His face was contorted and his eyes were dark and menacing. Rod actually feared for his life and was thankful that Franklin grabbed Ronnie in a bear hug and held him tightly as he squirmed and kicked himself to exhaustion, all the while screaming threats in Rod's direction. All the other guys were rolling around on the ground, twisted into various postures of uncontrollable laughter.

The day was saved when Mr. Winston arrived to see what all the fuss was about and quickly restored order. Even he could not avoid a brief snicker when the story came out. He made a mental note to file this one away for future use.

Later in the evening, Ronnie proved that he was a sport after all when he slapped Rod on the back (a little too hard, maybe) and stated: "How the devil did you come up with that one, Rod?" Rod just smiled to himself and enjoyed the moment. It was even worth the stinging he was now experiencing between his shoulder blades.

"I'm afraid I cannot reveal my source," he stated as he looked Ronnie squarely in the eyes.

As Ronnie walked away, shaking his head, Rod thought to himself, "Well, everything has a price, I guess, but it sure was worth it."

Chapter 12
Tall Tales

Gramma glanced out the window and saw Gramps and the two youngsters lounging in the shade of the pecan tree, Gramps in the hammock as usual and the kids seated at his side. She was amazed that they never seemed to tire of his company. Well, better that they keep out of my way, she thought. I never can seem to get much done with them underfoot all day. She did enjoy having them around for their summer visits, though and made sure that she spent her share of time with them as well.

She especially loved to take them on shopping trips where she could show them off to her friends. Oh, some of them had grand kids, too but she always thought hers were just a cut above the others. She surely did not begrudge Gramps his time with them. He wasn't getting any younger and they always seemed to make him want to act like a young man again. So she continued with her cleaning and decided not to interrupt for the moment.

Gramps was reminiscing about the good old days of his boyhood. It seemed to Rod and Ellie that things were a whole lot better back then. Even though they had to walk ten miles to school each day in the snow (it sure must have snowed more back then, they thought), the everyday things seemed to be much better. Movies only cost a quarter, soft drinks were a nickel and gas was only

25 cents per gallon. What they weren't told and did not think to ask was why, if things were so much better, they had changed.

Much later in their lives, they became familiar with 'selective memory' realizing that people tend to remember the good things and push bad memories to the side. One of Gramps' fondest memories was of the tall tales which made the rounds in the neighborhood he grew up in. He was telling the kids about some of them now.

He had begun, "Did I ever tell you kids about the Tall Tale Contest we had one time? Some people from the Chamber of Commerce thought it would be a good idea to use the favorite past time of the old timers to raise money to help pay the Chamber's operating expenses. Since there seemed to be an ongoing unofficial contest to see who could come up with the biggest whopper or to pull the best practical joke, why not use the natural talent of the locals to the Chamber's advantage?"

"It had gotten so bad with the old boys around town that you could hardly carry on a conversation without wondering if you were not about to be made the butt of some joke or to be told a flat lie."

"So the contest was organized and ran for several years, giving these pranksters a golden opportunity to exhibit their skills. For most, it was simply a competition to determine who was the champion liar of the county. But calling it a 'Liars Contest' seemed too offensive to be associated with the Chamber's image so the more acceptable title of 'Tall Tales Contest' was used, as though giving it a more acceptable name would excuse the liars for their sins."

"The first such contest was the best one. A time was

set and admission charged to hear those bold enough to stand in front of an audience and speak their falsehoods. The event was well attended, the local folk apparently enjoying a good poke in the ribs"

"There may have been other motivations, as well. With the perpetrators now out in the open, the populace could rest easy, at least for that night, knowing that whatever was said was not to be believed. Also, it was an opportunity to identify the jokesters and gain some inkling of the material they were constantly developing for future use at an opportune time."

"However, as witness to several of these contests and a participant in a couple of them myself, I am convinced that the speakers do not always use their best material for the contest, instead holding their best stuff for situations in which an unsuspecting victim can be duped. The small, monetary reward for winning, even when coupled with the recognition of being the county's best liar, did not compare with the prestige garnered in the community when a 'good one' was pulled off. It would be the talk of the town for several weeks after it happened or at least until it was bested. Many a conversation would be begun ... 'Did you hear what Ole Paul did to Homer the other day? Man, you shoulda been there...' And the stories usually got better with each telling."

"Can you tell us about some of them, Gramps?" Ellie asked.

"Sure can. In fact I was just remembering a couple of classic tall tales which were told during the first competition."

"That would be great, Gramps!" Rod agreed.

"Well, you kids have heard me talk about Old John Hicks before, haven't you? He had one of the best stories that night although he didn't win. That honor went to another local legend, 'Fessor Lowrey, a retired school teacher. I even had one myself, although I didn't even place. I thought it was pretty funny but I guess the judges didn't agree. Which one do you want to hear?"

"Why can't you tell all of them?" Ellie asked.

"Yeah, why not?" Rod agreed.

"Oh, I guess I could but it'll take a while."

"We're not going anywhere," Ellie stated matter of factly.

"I'm not either," Gramps said. "So why not?" He was certainly willing if they were.

"Since you're already familiar with Old John Hicks, I'll begin with him. I've already told you something about his character and personality. He was a bonafide, tongue-in-cheek prankster. Old John was prone to tall tales and 'exaggerations'. The listener would always have to be on guard for the 'hook' in each story."

"With a deathly serious look on his face, he once told me about a summer which had such a severe drought that every catfish he caught had to be dusted for fleas. On another occasion, he told me about a bass he'd caught which was so big, the snapshot of it weighed two pounds. He said that fish was caught very near the same spot where he had caught another one so big, that when he went back the next day, water was still running into the hole he had pulled him out of! Not all his stories glorified his own fishing prowess, though. One day he told me about a friend of his, Poppa Joe Seagler, who showed him a prized photo album labeled, *Ten Pound Bass I Have Caught.* Mr. John had eagerly opened up this treasured possession only to find fifty blank pages. Poppa Joe thought this was about the funniest joke he'd ever pulled although I doubt that."

"Unfortunately, Old John was much like many fine athletes who have acquired the label 'underrated'. He was as skilled a practitioner of the tall tale or other stories containing 'hooks' as anyone. He was just very quiet and understated. He never wanted to call attention to himself. Therefore, he never received the credit due him. But that suited him just fine. He was just as happy for the winner as he would have been if it had been him. In fact, I believe he was even more so."

"Old John's contribution to the Tall Tales Contest on that first night was one of his best in my opinion and should have won the first prize. I still have it on video tape and would love to show it to you sometime. But, for now, I'll just tell it to you as he told it, to the best of my recollection. Old John spoke in a quiet, barely audible voice as he began his tale:

"'Back when I was just a young man, there was a grist mill located outside of town where all the local farmers took their corn to be ground into meal for cooking. It was a good fishing spot because little fish would gather underneath the floor to feast on the droppings which would fall through the cracks in the plank floor. Of course, bigger fish would come to eat the little fish and yet bigger fish would come in to eat them. It was not unusual for big bass and catfish to be caught from the waters surrounding the mill.'"

"'Well, one day, me and my friend Wilson were fishing there when Wilson hooked a bass so big he couldn't turn him and the fish swam directly into the turbines and jammed the mill wheel so badly several of the gears were displaced and the huge wheel came to a halt with a horrible screeching noise sounding something like a train braking hard. With the gears out of kilter, the wheel finally began to turn again but there was a problem. Mr. Hortman, who operated the mill hollered out the window that we needed to do something because the wheel was now running backwards. We didn't know what else to do so we beached the boat and ran up the steps and opened the water gate, releasing a torrent of water and forcing the gears back into place with a loud 'thunk'! The wheel began running in the right direction again."

"Me and Wilson went on up to check on Mr. Hortman. He was fit to be tied. Not that any permanent damage had been done to the machinery, though. What he was upset about was that the wheel running in reverse had *unground* a good bit of corn before he could get it stopped. He would now have to regrind it since he had promised it that day. He would have to stay late and would not be paid any extra because he worked strictly on volume. We offered our sympathies but did not see how we could do anything further so we went home."

"The next day, Wilson was in town and went to *The Greasy Spoon*, a local eatery where the men of the town went to swap tales and espouse their own personal remedies for solving all of the nation's ills. It was in this environment that fish often grew to proportions heretofore unknown in the annals of the sport and no deer less than ten points and two hundred pounds had ever been taken."

"Wilson sauntered in just as Mr. Woods, the proprietor, was completing his retelling of the previous days' events at Hortman's Mill. Wilson heard him say, '…and before they could get the wheel turned around, it had unground three bushels of corn.'"

"Of course, upon spotting Wilson, an actual eye witness, the men wanted verification of the story. Not wanting to ever be accused of spreading falsehoods or exaggerations, Wilson quickly complied.

"'Well boys,' he said in his most serious tone, 'I was there so you can take it from me. Mr. Woods is telling an outright lie.'"

"'Yeah, I thought he was lyin',' one man shouted. Everyone else nodded their agreement with that statement."

"Nodding his assent with a smug look on his face and a twinkle in his eye, Wilson assured them, 'Yessir boys, that's an outright lie. I know for a fact that wheel only unground a little over two bushels of corn!'"

" Of course, that revelation brought forth a round of hoots and hollers as nearly everyone shouted 'Told you so' or 'I knew it'."

"That's pretty good, Gramps!" Rod chuckled.

"Yeah, if that didn't win, I'd sure like to hear the one that did."

"All in good time, kids, all in good time. I'm going to save the best for last. First, I want to tell you my story. It's not exactly a tall tale since it was published in the local newspaper as a true story, but it was funny and required a little acting ability for the best effect so I think it was note-worthy."

"Well, let's hear it," the kids shouted in unison.

"All right then," Gramps agreed as he got into his tale telling posture. The far away, dreamy look came into his eyes as his memory cells began connecting to put the story together. "Let's see, it was a story about a brick layer who was trying to relate to the insurance company the source of his numerous injuries in order to file a claim on his workman's comp insurance. That's insurance which pays the medical bills for people injured on their jobs. I'll try to tell it in his own words:

"'I'm a bricklayer by trade. Although I have been called lazy by some, I prefer to think of myself as a man who looks for ways to make hard jobs easier. That's what I was doing on the day of the accident.'"

"'We had finished work for the day on a three-story building and the foreman noted that we had brought up more bricks than were needed and I found myself being recruited to move the pile of bricks back down to the ground. The lift truck we had used to get them up there was a rental unit which had already been returned. The foreman did not want to incur any additional expense and saw no reason I could not carry them down one load at a time.'"

"'Judging from the size of the pile, it would probably take eight or nine trips and I sure did not look forward to that ordeal. That's when my brainstorm hit. I noticed that a pulley which had been used to bring various tools up to the workers was still in place, attached to a couple of reinforced two-by-fours suspended over the edge of the building, the rope dangling from it reaching all the way to the ground. Nearby was an empty fifty-five gallon drum which, on cold days, was used to house a fire for warmth. It looked to be just the right size to hold the excess bricks.'"

"'Using a drill bit, I quickly punched two holes into the side of the barrel just below the rim and tied the rope firmly to the barrel. I ran down to the ground and tied the loose end of the rope to a nearby oak tree with one of those knots you can untie by snatching on one end of the rope.'"

"'I then went back, swung the barrel out over the edge and filled it with the bricks. Someone later estimated the weight of the bricks and barrel combined to be in excess of three hundred pounds. This is an important fact because I only weigh about one-sixty-five myself.'"

"'I then went back down to the ground, wrapped the loose end of the rope around my wrist, braced myself with feet apart, firmly planted and snatched the loose end of the rope.'"

"'I was immediately snatched off the ground and began a rapid ascent to the top of the building, my progress interrupted only by the barrel of bricks which collided with my head at the second floor. That explains my fractured skull.'"

"'I somehow got past the bricks and continued upward until my fingers were jammed two knuckles deep into the pulley. That would explain the two broken fingers on my right hand.'"

"'At the same time my hand reached the pulley, the barrel reached the ground with a loud crash, the bottom falling out, leaving the bricks piled on the ground. Minus the bricks, the barrel weighed only fifty pounds. Remember, my weight is one sixty-five.'"

"'I started my descent as the barrel was snatched off the ground much as I had been earlier. We met again at the second floor. That accounts for the severe abrasions on my shins and my broken ankle.'"

"'I again somehow got past the barrel and was soon deposited flat on my back onto the pile of bricks, explaining the three ruptured vertebrae in my lower back.'"

"'Lying there on my back, dazed and semi-conscious, the barrel hanging directly above my head, I made one final mistake. I let go of the rope! I don't remember anything after that.'"

"Gramps, what a horrible story," Ellie cried as her softer side took over.

"Maybe so, but you have to admit, it's pretty funny, huh Gramps," Rod was grinning at the mental images the story provoked. "Is it really true?"

"I don't know, but I sure don't doubt it. People are always doing one crazy thing or another. Haven't you ever watched *America's Funniest Home Videos?* It kinda reminds me of some of the foolish things those folks do."

"Yeah, you're right. I can't believe some folks can be so dumb," Rod agreed.

"Well, what about the winner of the contest? Aren't you gonna tell us about it?" Ellie was insistent.

"Of course I am. I promised didn't I? Just gimme a minute to recollect just how it went. I already told you the tall tale winner was 'Fessor Lowrey. He was also a soft spoken fellow but, having been a school teacher, he was naturally a bit more eloquent than Old John. He always tried to interject his stories with some sort of object lesson and this one was no exception. Again, I'll try to relate his tale in his own words:

"'I was raised on a farm way back in the country and us kids had to help with the chores as soon as we were old enough. It was a rare occasion when we were allowed a day off and when we were, we took full advantage of it. Well, one day my daddy was going into town for some business and I asked if he minded if I went fishing down in the swamp. He said it was OK but I needed to be sure to take my hatchet with me. Now, I wondered what use I would have for a hatchet on a fishing trip but we were taught not to question our parents and so I stuck the hatchet into my belt and was on my way.'"

"'Now, this swamp was so far back in the woods that it seldom was visited by humans and rumors were that there were some mighty big mosquitoes in the area. I was soon to find that out for myself.'"

"' I was just getting ready to bait my hook for my first cast when I heard this very loud buzzing noise and looked up to see a mosquito the size of a jet plane coming right for me.'"

"'My only hope was to dodge behind a big oak tree just as the mosquito was about to impale me on his beak. He hit the tree so hard that his beak went completely through and was sticking out about a foot on my side. I quickly got my hatchet out and bent his beak to the side so he could not withdraw it.'"

"'He began kicking and thrashing about but could not extract his beak. After about an hour he finally kicked himself to death. You won't believe it but his thrashing about ended up clearing five acres of land, on which we raised some of the best cotton you ever saw for many years after that.'"

"'Now you kids in the audience need to remember that when your mama and daddy tell you to do something, you should do it because you never know when they are telling you something for your own good which you would have never figured out for yourself. Even now, whenever I go the swamp fishing, I always take my hatchet!'"

"Now I've kept you kids' attention far too long. You need to go and see if your Gramma needs help with anything" Gramps attempted to dismiss them with a hug.

"Before we go, Gramps, can you tell us what's the difference between a tall tale and an outright lie?" Rod wanted to know.

"That's a good question, son. Some folks have a hard time distinguishing them, even as adults. The best thing I can tell you is that if you tell a lie, intending for someone to take it for the truth, then that's a lie and should not be told. On the other hand, a tall tale or a story with an obvious 'hook' which the listener will recognize at the appropriate time is acceptable so long as no one is hurt by it."

"It's not always real easy to tell the difference. If you're not sure if your intentions were understood, you should be sure to tell the listener that you were joking." It was time for his nap, now and he knew he could never give it his best effort as long as the kids were around.

"Thanks, Gramps," they shouted back over their shoulders as they ran to look for Gramma.

Chapter 13
The Big Game

"Quiet, ladies, Roddie's coming up next," Gramps advised Gramma and her friend Emma. The Little League game they were attending was winding down and Rod's team, the Reds were down by one run in the bottom half of the last inning. Rod was not having the best day of his career, having struck out twice and grounded back to the pitcher. Normally a better than average hitter, he may have been feeling a little extra pressure today, with his grandparents present for the first time this season. Rod was on one knee in the on-deck circle and trying his best to focus on the pitcher but could not resist a quick glance over his shoulder to see if Gramps was paying attention. He was encouraged to see that Gramps was not only paying attention, but to prove it, he quickly gave Rod a "thumbs up" signal.

Rod couldn't keep a small grin from splitting his lips. He knew that Gramps was on his side even if he struck out every time. He felt like he just had to do something good this time to reward the old man for his patience. He had made a couple of sparkling fielding plays from his second base position, but in his mind that didn't mean anything now unless he could produce at the plate. There were now two outs in the bottom of the sixth with no one on base. Unless Scotty could get on, he would not get a chance to redeem himself, at least not in this game anyway.

He watched with a feeling of growing despair as Scotty took a second called strike. They were now down to their last strike and it looked like the opposing pitcher had all the confidence in the world and he went into his windup again. The ball became a blur as Scotty swung weakly and dribbled a foul down the first base line.

"You've got him now," the Braves coach shouted. "See, he can't get around on your fast ball!"

Suddenly, Rod heard his own coach yell, "Time, Blue!" Everything became very quiet as coach Simms called Scotty to the sidelines.

Scotty came over slowly, dreading what the coach may have to say. Coach Simms himself even seemed a little uneasy with the situation. "Now look, Scotty," he began. "I've been studying this guy's tendencies during the course of this game and he has gone to his change every time he's been ahead in the count with two strikes. Our guys have been waving at the floater, so far out in front they've almost fallen down with their swings. I'm betting that's what they're going to throw now. It's worked all game so why not? Anyway, I want you to stay back and wait for the change. If I'm wrong and he throws a fast ball, I'll take all the blame."

Scotty was not at all sure the coach was right. It would be just like this pitcher to fool everyone and come with his heater, leaving Scotty standing there with his bat on his shoulder. But he knew in his heart that he could not catch up to the fast ball anyway so he reluctantly agreed.

"OK, coach," he said meekly and stepped back into the box.

Before he could even get settled into his stance, the

pitcher began his motion. It was very exaggerated and Scotty suddenly knew the changeup was coming. He kept his weight on his back foot and was rewarded with the sight of the lollipop floating toward him. As it got nearer, he began his forward stride and lashed at the ball as it got even with the plate. A loud "crack" was followed by the sight of the ball streaking over the third baseman's head toward the left field corner. Scotty rounded first and began sprinting toward second expecting to have to slide in ahead of the throw. Instead, he heard the third base coach yelling "Three, Scotty, Three" He barely slowed as he rounded second and headed toward third just as he saw the left fielder come up throwing.

The throw looked like a good one and he knew it was going to be a close play. He heard the coach shouting, "Get down, get down!" as he began his slide. The third baseman fielded the ball cleanly and slapped his leg with a tag just as his foot connected with the bag.

"Safe!" came the call from the umpire.

The call was drowned out by loud screaming from the Braves' side and cheering from the Reds' side. The Braves coach was livid, knowing the game was over if his team had gotten the call. Instead, they were now in danger of being tied up and having to go extra innings.

He gave the umpire a piece of his mind and then called time out to speak to his pitcher. "That's OK, Devin," he told him. "He just got lucky on that one. This next guy hasn't put a bat on the ball all day. All you gotta do is get him and the game's over. You can do it, son. I'm counting on you."

Devin nodded. He was supremely confident himself as he took the ball and stepped to the rubber.

Rod was keenly aware of the pressure of the situation.

Get the run in and tie the game and he was a hero. Fail, and he was the goat. He suddenly remembered something Gramps had told him many times, the most recent time being yesterday. Rod had been upset because he had been unable to beat one of his friends at a video game. He had lost four straight games and was well on his way to losing the fifth, when he noticed Gramps watching from the doorway. As the game concluded with the same result as before, Rod became angry and threw his controller to the floor in frustration. He looked up to see that Gramps had left the room. He was immediately ashamed of the way he had acted.

Later that evening, Gramps came into Rod's room just before bedtime. "Rod, I just wanted you to know that I was not particularly pleased with the way you acted today."

"I know, Gramps, but I just couldn't beat Ryan, no matter how well I played and it just got me angry!"

"Well, son, you'll find as you go along in this life that there will always be somebody better at something than you. That should not frustrate you because I'm sure there are many things you are better at than Ryan. Does he get mad when you beat him?"

"No, sir. In fact, when I stop to think about it, he usually just grins and says something like he better practice more if he wants to compete with me."

"Well, that's the right attitude. The most important thing is that, when the contest is over, you know in your heart that you have done your best. If you can honestly say 'yes' then you have nothing to be ashamed of."

Gramps' words came back to him now and Rod resolved that he was going to do his very best and if that wasn't good enough, he was going to congratulate Devin on a game well played. But not just yet, he thought. First, he's got to get me out.

Rod stepped into the box with grim determination written all over his face. In the stands, Gramps said to no one in particular, "Now ya'll are gonna' see what the boy's made of"

Rod scooped a handful of dirt into his palms, rubbed them together and took a determined stance. The first pitch fooled him completely. It was a curve which caused him to buckle his knees and step backward as the ball dropped neatly into the catcher's mitt.

"Strike One" came the call.

Two fastballs barely missed the outside corner as Devin tried to take advantage of Rod's previous step into the bucket. The next fast ball split the middle.

"Strike two" the umpire bellowed.

Rod's stomach churned. One more of those and I'm history, he thought.

"Time, Blue", he heard coach Simms call. He ambled over to the baseline and awaited his coaches advice. "Rod, his tendency is to throw the change in this situation. I can't believe he'll do any different this time."

"But coach, the last time he tried it Scotty ripped it," Rod countered.

"Yeah, but he knows that was just luck and he's going to try it again. I'd stake my rep on it."

"I don't think so coach. He's struck me out twice on fast balls and I'm convinced he'll try it again." Rod argued.

"Rod, I'm the coach and have a great deal more experience than you in these situations, so I want you to listen to me. Get ready for the change."

Rod was not happy with these instructions but felt he

had no choice. He knew he was right. The fates smiled upon him as the pitcher would up and Rod kept his weight back as a fastball left the pitcher's hand.

"Ball Three" came the umpire's call as the ball barely missed inside. The count was now three and two.

"Now you're ready, son. Now you're ready" Rod heard Gramps' encouragement and he knew he was as ready as he would ever be. "I may fail," he thought to himself, "but I'm not going to give up! I'm going to give it my best shot."

He cocked the bat and stepped into the box, looking as though he could hardly wait for the pitch. Devin looked just as confident as he rocked into his wind. It was again, the very exaggerated motion, the same one which always preceded his changeup. Somehow, Rod knew better! His eyes were clear as they picked up the sphere as it left the pitcher's hand on a line destined to carry it quickly into the catcher's mitt and victory.

With a quick stride and flip of his wrists, Rod put the bat squarely on the ball in front of the plate.

The hush which had fallen over the stands as the sequence was begun, turned to bedlam as the ball began its high arc toward center field. The Braves center fielder shouted, "I got it" and began to retreat as the ball gained altitude. It that appeared he had plenty of room to haul it in. He hesitantly retreated two more steps before his back made contact with the fence just as the ball tipped off the end of his glove and landed a foot on the other side.

Most of the fans could not tell if he had caught it or not. The second base umpire rushed to the outfield to make the call. The empty glove told the tale.

The Reds' stands erupted with wild cheering as Rod slowly rounded the bases, tears in his eyes and a grin on his face. He leaped the last three feet onto home plate and was immediately covered by a mass of humanity composed of his teammates. He barely felt the pummeling he received. He could not remember a time when he had felt so good!

In the stands, saying little other than "I told you, so" Gramps appeared as though he would burst with pride.

Much later that evening, before the children were put to bed, Gramps paid a short visit to Rod's bedroom. A new plastic ball-stand on his dresser held a baseball signed by twelve boys. The shiny plastic stand appeared for all the world to be pure gold. As far as Rod was concerned, it would not have meant any more to him if it had been.

"Just wanted to say good night, Rod and tell you how proud I was of you today."

"Thanks, Gramps. I really was as surprised as anyone to hit a game-winning homer."

"I'm not talking about that," Gramps said. "Not many others noticed, but I saw you go over and console Devin as he was crying about losing the game for his team"

"Oh, you saw that did you? He looked so sad."

"It was a great display of sportsmanship and meant more to me than ten homers would have. And you want to know something else?'

"What's that, Gramps?"

"I asked several people how many times you struck out today. And not one of them could tell me. 'Who cares', they'd say. And they were right, you know. Failures are soon forgotten unless you quit. You didn't quit and that's what matters most and what people will remember."

"Thanks, Gramps. That means a lot to me," Rod said

quietly as he took one last look at his prize before Gramps turned out the light and eased from the room.

Chapter 14

The Bike Wreck on Breezy Hill

Gramps had begun anticipating the summer visit from the kids for several weeks now and had become more and more irritable as the days passed and he became anxious for their arrival. Even though he knew the exact date they would be there, he had begun looking down the long drive every day, thinking that, just maybe, they would come early this year. He should have known better as the date school ended for the summer was not something likely to change. Nevertheless, he couldn't help himself and his anticipation grew in proportion to his disappointment.

At last, the day was here and they were scheduled to arrive right after lunch today. As Gramma prepared his usual tomato sandwich, she noticed a twinkle in his eye and asked if he was all right.

"'Course I'm all right," he bellowed, "Rod and Ellie are coming today and I've got some juicy tales for 'em."

"I'll bet you do," Gramma replied, "But I hope you give 'em a little time to get settled before you start boring them to death with your stories."

"Boring?" Gramps roared. "Let me tell you, woman, the kids LOVE my stories and I love tellin' 'em, so you just need to tend to your knittin' and leave us before a while. There'll be plenty of time for them to unpack and settle in."

Gramma knew better than to try and reason with him so she decided to pursue the subject no further. She knew they would want some iced lemonade so she began cutting and squeezing some lemons.

An hour or so later, she heard the dogs begin barking and knew that company had arrived. It was an indisputable fact the no one could sneak up to the Skidmore's house without the dogs announcing their arrival well in advance. Sure enough, she looked down the drive and there, amidst a moving cloud of dust, she saw their son's black Ford sedan bearing him and the kids to their doorstep. She started for the front door but Gramps beat her there by two full strides, flinging open the door stepping out onto the front veranda. His face was split by the biggest grin in four counties.

"Hey, Gramma!" he was shouting, "Look who's here. What a surprise!"

The car had not fully stopped before Rod and Ellie threw open the car doors and ran to his open arms, each wanting to be the first to get a hug. They hit him simultaneously and almost knocked him off his feet.

"Whoa! Hold on there kids," Gramps protested, as he was wrapped in arms and legs.

"Let an old man steady himself before y'all knock him over." Totally ignoring his protests, they covered him with hugs and kisses until their father gently pulled them off.

"Hello, Dad," Ernest said, as he gripped Gramps hand and shook it vigorously. "It sure is good to see you." It had been five months since his parents had come to the city for a Christmas visit. It seemed to them both much longer. Since the son's promotion, their visits had become less frequent, a situation neither was happy with, but which neither could find a solution. So they saw each other as much as they could and tried to make the best of each visit.

"Come on in the house, son," Gramps urged. "Take a load off. Gramma's got some lemonade chilled and I know it'll be mighty good on a hot day like today."

"OK, Dad, but just for awhile, you understand. I've got to get back to the city for a special dinner tonight."

"I understand, son. Don't worry about a thing. Gramma and me will take care of the young'uns."

An hour and a half later, after unpacking the kids' stuff and visiting for a spell, Ernest was on the road back to his home. Among the kids' "stuff" he had left was a pair of new bicycles, which they had gotten for their birthdays a couple of months ago. They had had little opportunity to ride their bikes in the city, with the crowded streets and dangerous drivers, but now they were in the country and there were miles of uncongested roads on which to try them out. And they were anxious to do so. They had ridden them around in the yard for a couple of hours before dark, but soon were ready for some longer forays.

Gramps finally called out to them, "You kids put those bikes up for the night. It's getting too dark and I don't want you running into any of my trees! Tomorrow, we'll see about you taking a much longer ride, OK?"

They were a little tired from the days' activity anyway and Gramma had supper almost ready, so they were agreeable to call it a night.

It was eight o'clock in the morning of the following day and breakfast was finished. Rod and Ellie reminded Gramps that he had promised them a longer ride today and they were ready to go. Gramps told them to give him just a few more minutes as he needed to fetch something from the barn. They reluctantly agreed but showed their impatience by riding in circles around the yard. Five minutes later Gramps emerged from the barn pushing the oldest bicycle they had ever seen. If it had ever had paint, it was long since worn off. Rust was showing on almost all the frame and the seat was worn and frayed. The spokes were missing in several places as well. Its overall appearance was shabby at best and a "death trap" at worst. The only thing new about it was the tires. They wondered aloud about that.

"Well, you see, after you young'uns went to bed last night, I decided that you blame well weren't going on no ride today without me, so I went down to the hardware store and got me some new tires and a can of oil. Didn't have time to do nothin' fancy to improve its looks but at least I wanted it to be safe. So here it is. The bike of my boyhood. Fifty years old if it's a day!"

Rod and Ellie were astonished to say the least. Rod piped up, "You're not seriously thinking about riding that thing are you?" he asked.

"Why not," Gramps retorted. "I bet it'll hold up as well as ya'll's new ones with all their fancy hand brakes, ten gears and such. It has a very simple formula for moving. You press the pedals and it moves forward. Not much can go wrong with that."

Ellie looked at Rod and they nodded. "OK, Gramps," she called, "let's see what it can do. But don't go complaining when you have to walk back pushing that piece of junk!"

Gramps snorted. "We'll see who has to walk back, young lady. Now let's stop this yammerin' and get this show on the road." With that, he hopped onto the seat and began to pedal furiously down the drive. He was a good hundred yards ahead before they could mount up and follow.

Although Gramps had a healthy lead, they began to slowly gain on him as they shifted into higher gears while steadily increasing their speed. Within a mile they drew abreast of him and had to slow their pace to match his. Gramps abruptly turned off the gravel road onto a dirt road, whose surface was not unlike the washboard Gramma sometimes used. The ride became very rough; a teeth jarring experience, which they soon began to hate.

"Gramps, let's get back on the pavement where we can enjoy the ride without rattling our brains, OK?" Rod called.

"In a minute," Gramps responded, "but first I want to show you something. Just follow me."

They obediently followed.

Within five more minutes Gramps stopped in the middle of the road, which was at the top of a very steep grade. As they sat and gazed down the incline, it was obvious that, near the bottom, the road took a sharp left and could no longer be seen past the curve.

"I hope we're not going down that hill," Ellie pleaded. Rod, too expressed his feelings on the matter, blurting out, "Me too, Gramps. That looks like suicide."

"Don't worry kids," Gramps consoled, "We're not going to try that today. I just wanted you to see the scene of what was referred to for years as the *Breezy Hill Bike Wreck.* My old buddy Pork Campbell was the victim at the time. But he eventually gained the admiration of all the boys by merely surviving the fall that put him into a category all by himself. You see, no one before had ever made it all the way around the curve without falling. He came within thirty or so yards of completing the run. Oh, he paid dearly, but in his eyes, the recognition he received made it all worthwhile. Let's sit a spell under this old oak tree and I'll tell you all about it."

As they pulled the bikes off the road, Gramps broke out a knapsack into which Gramma had packed a thermos of lemonade and a dozen chocolate chip cookies she'd baked last night. They found comfortable spots as Gramps began his story:

"I'm referring to a particularly nasty spill Pork took fifty or so years ago, right on this very spot in the road. This was a slope which had been a challenge to neighborhood boys for years. Not only was the grade extremely steep, there was also the ninety-degree turn at the bottom which no one could take at full speed."

"Many had tried, as the deep gouges in the clay bank attested. The stories of each unfortunate boys' failure and subsequent injuries had become the stuff of local legend. Jerry Hooker had come closest to making it a few years back, but even he had crashed at the last instant, clipping a low hanging tree branch, knocking out several teeth. A second mortgage was required for his father to pay for the orthodontist's work. At least he ended up with a great set of teeth, though."

"Pork, though, being Pork was undaunted by the mishaps of the various contenders to be the first to make it. He had worked on his bike for weeks, getting the brakes adjusted to a fine degree and making sure his tires had good tread. He had advertised for weeks the date on which he was to make his attempt so a good crowd had gathered on that Saturday morning as he arrived. Jerry Hooker, showing off his new smile, wished him well, although he secretly doubted he had any chance. When he was convinced he had milked the preliminaries for all they were worth, Pork, mounted "Old faithful" and pulled to the starting point. A chant broke out, 'Let's go Pork!, Let's go Pork! Let's go Pork!' It became so loud, I was told it could be heard clear into town."

"With a huge grin on his face, Pork pushed off and immediately accelerated to maximum speed. He had not calculated that is weight would be a factor, but it surely was. Pork had no choice but to try to keep the bike under control by careful braking. This proved useless as the tires gained no traction and the bike began to fishtail wildly. Somehow he kept it in the center of the road all the way to the curve. Then, disaster! The chain came off! When Pork pushed down on the pedals and felt no resistance, he knew immediately what had happened, setting off panic mode in his brain. He knew there was no way he could control his speed with no brakes. He also knew that unless he could find some way to decrease his speed, he was doomed. He immediately began to drag his feet which had no effect but to enlarge the holes in the bottom of his tennis shoes and scrape skin off the bottoms of his feet.. He quickly abandoned this strategy and decided to steer to the shallowest ditch he could find in order to minimize the damage. As he went off the main road, the front wheel hit a six inch cross rut, stopping it immediately and causing the bike to flip forward, throwing Pork over the handlebars."

"As he was separated from the bike, he executed his best swan dive, landing on his chest with arms forward to break his fall. As he skidded on the hard-packed Georgia clay, a trail of skin was left in his wake. Finally stopping two feet short of a huge oak tree, he counted his blessings for this small favor."

"He soon realized, though that this thought was a little premature. As he sat up and began assessing the huge raw, skinless areas of his chest and arms, the bicycle crashed into him from behind, one pedal and the tip of the handlebar each producing new puncture wounds in his back and some unknown part producing an egg sized knot on his head. He was astonished to be still alive and conscious but the pain assured him he was. A huge cheer went up from the crowd as he sat up and began to crawl back to the road. He was able to actually walk on his own back to the top of the hill where he was cheered some more. The county sheriff had arrived by that time and gave him a lift back to his home. Pork later swore that the pain of his injuries was nothing compared to the pain produced by the alcohol poured into each open wound by his mother, a firm believer in the principle of 'First, the wound must be cleaned.' The sound of his tortured screams were talked about by the neighbors for years to come."

"So, you see, kids", Gramps continued, "Bicycles can be a lot of fun, but like many other pleasures, you must use good judgement and plain old common sense to fully appreciate them. I hope this story will teach you to think before you act. Most youg'uns don't consider the consequences of their actions until after they act. 'Course, then it's too late. So, what I'm telling you is to use the good sense God gave you and you'll save yourselves a lot of heartache."

"We will, Gramps," they said in unison. Only time would tell whether they were sincere.

Chapter 15
Walking the Creek

Rod and Ellie burst out of the edge of the woods and made a mad dash toward the little creek which meandered within a mile of Gramps' house. Each was determined to be the first to reach the cool waters of the "swimmin' hole", their favorite place to beat the oppressive heat of yet another typical summer day in Georgia. The temperature hovered in the high nineties and sweat had covered their bodies as they hiked with Gramps following close behind, encouraging them not to get too far ahead.

For the most part, they had obliged him but with the prize in sight, they could constrain themselves no longer. They simply had to have some relief. They hit the water almost simultaneously, with Rob perhaps a half-step ahead, throwing up a plume of cool spray accompanied by Ellie's squeals of delight. As their bodies were immersed in the cool creek water, Gramps trudged down to the edge and smiled knowingly. He had been experiencing the same reaction with every visit to the creek since his childhood many years before. He eased his tired feet into the knee deep water and then just sat down on the gravelly sandbar where he could keep a close eye on the frolicking youngsters.

The creek had changed little in the fifty or so years since he had been a boy and enjoyed its cool waters much as Rod and Ellie were doing now. "What could be better than this," he thought to himself as he absorbed the beauty of his surroundings. His brief reverie was abruptly interrupted as a spray of water pelted his face. Rod grinned as he unleashed another burst from his water pistol. His aim was true and Gramps was totally soaked.

"Oh, so you want war, do you?" Gramps roared as he sprang up from his seat and yanked his own full water pistol from his belt.

He was still pretty nimble for a man of seventy. Gramps had secretly filled it with crushed ice before leaving home and its contents now consisted of ice cold water. He sent a stream straight into Rod's back, producing a high-pitched screech almost as shrill as those Ellie was famous for.

"No fair, Gramps!" Rod whined. "You didn't tell us you had a Super Soaker".

"I didn't get old and not learn a few things along the way. And I ain't told you kids half of what I know yet. So watch and learn. Some day you may be as smart as me."

"Yeah, Rod, you dummy," Ellie chimed in.

"I hope you don't think you're any smarter, Miss Priss," Gramps shouted as he sent another stream, this one catching Ellie squarely on her exposed shoulder.

Ellie eluded further damage by diving into the pool, surfacing more than twenty feet away, out of range of the icy stream.

Gramps immediately resumed his attack on Rod, who had not moved while Ellie was receiving her dose. His failure to anticipate further attacks was rewarded by an icy blast to his face. He quickly joined Ellie a safe distance from the old man, who was now shooting a stream into his mouth, quenching the thirst he had developed on the walk from the house.

The expression on his face said, "I dare you to retaliate!"

Rod and Ellie quickly conferred and came up with a plan. Each began a slow but steady flanking movement, knowing Gramps could not shoot in two directions at the same time.

Again, they under-estimated his resourcefulness. He quickly saw through their strategy and bided his time, waiting for the simultaneous attack he knew was forthcoming. As soon as Rod nodded his head at Ellie, a move that Gramps correctly guessed was their pre-determined signal, he pulled a second Super Soaker from his pocket and gave them each a long blast as they rushed his position.

Squealing as the cold water once again found its mark on their bare skin, they continued their onslaught and were soon positioned on each side of the old man, giving him a full dose of the medicine he had dished out. He was quickly overwhelmed and could only bow his head to shield his face from further discomfort. Fortunately, each of the combatants had now run out of ammunition and all collapsed in a pile in the shallow water, their laughter ringing through the forest.

Gramps picked up each in turn, tossing them into the creek in a jumble of knees and elbows. They surfaced in the waist deep water, spluttering and tossing their heads to clear their vision. By this time Gramps had retreated far up the bank and sat down under a spreading oak, which provided ample shade. He called a truce, declaring the battle a draw and began rummaging through the back pack he had deposited nearby. He produced a trio of ham sandwiches, a bag of potato chips and three sodas.

“I declare,” he announced, “walkin’ two miles and fightin’ a couple of tigers has plum wore me out. I think we all deserve a little rest and relaxation, don’t ya’ll?”

They answered by plopping down beside him and quickly popping the tops of two of the sodas which they began to guzzle. The ham sandwiches and potato chips were quickly disposed of and the three of them lay on their backs on the soft grass in total contentment.

Within a few minutes Rod and Ellie began to hear sounds coming from Gramps resembling snores. They giggled as the sounds became louder and decided it was time for them to get the best of Gramps for a change. Rod picked a long stem of grass and began to bush it lightly under Gramps’ nose. He immediately snorted and slapped at his face as he tried to dislodge the fly he imagined was crawling across his nose. The kids giggled even louder. After several repetitions of this maneuver, Rod shifted the location of his attack to Gramps’ ears, producing a similar but more violent result. The children were now beside themselves with laughter as Gramps began unconsciously digging into first one ear, then the other, all the while snorting like some deranged hog.

Suddenly one of Gramps’ eyes popped open and he grabbed Rod and Ellie in a bear hug, growling loudly. At the same time, he began tickling each of them until he had them begging for mercy. “Thought you could pull one over on your old Gramps, did you?” he roared. “Well, you young whippersnappers will have to get up pretty early in the morning to outwit this old man.”

“Aw, Gramps, you knew it was Rod all the time, didn’t you?” Ellie seemed disappointed.

“No, not the whole time, just when he started digging in my ears and ya’lls laughter got a little too loud for me to sleep through. But I have to admit, you came up with a pretty good idea. Reminds of some of the good times me and my friends had on this very creek when we were not much older than you are now."

The kids saw the "look" come across the old man's face and knew he was about to launch into a tale. Their gazes were totally focused on his face. "What did ya'll do, Gramps," Rod asked.

"Oh, well, we didn't have the same toys you kids have now. We sure didn't have any 'Super Soakers' and not much of anything else. We had to make do with simple things like cane fishing poles and slingshots. Oh, and sometimes, one or two of us might get to bring our dad's shotgun or .22 rifle in case we saw a snake. Seems like there were a whole lot more snakes back then."

His brow knitted as he concentrated, trying to dredge from his memory banks some of the things he and his boyhood friends had done. Soon, his face relaxed as the memories slowly began to emerge from the deep recesses of his brain.

"Well, since we've got a little time to kill before we can get back into the water, I guess I can think of a few of our 'adventures'".

"Usually we'd get together on a Saturday morning with each kid bringing along his own stuff, prepared to spend the day on the creek. We would ride our bikes from home and meet at a pre-arranged spot about a mile from the creek and ride the final mile as a group. The group usually consisted of me and Pork and Weed, of course, with anywhere from three to five additional kids, depending upon who could get away and join us for the day."

"Since there were dozens of these trips scattered

throughout several years, I'm just going to tell you about one memorable trip in particular. On this trip, we were joined by the Jenkins brothers, Larry and Leroy, who had only one bike between them and had to ride together, not a very comfortable proposition, considering the mile ride to the creek was along an old abandoned logging road, which was rutted and full of rocks and limbs, creating a bone jarring, teeth rattling course which could hardly be endured without a series of whoops and screams as each successive bump was encountered."

"The Larsen boys were also along that day. They were identical twin brothers who were slightly more affluent than the rest of the group. They usually had new bikes each Christmas and were a little proud of the finer clothes they wore and the newer toys they always seemed to be getting. The guys in the group could easily identify Tom and Tim. To us they looked almost nothing alike. It constantly amazed others that we could so easily tell them apart as almost no one, other than their parents, could"

"Hank, a boy who lived with his grandmother across the road from us, also joined the group for the trip that day. Hank was somewhat of a loner, who was not just an only child, he was also adopted, which we never considered as a disadvantage, but was a circumstance with which he never seemed to be quite comfortable. He never talked about it much, but he always seemed to be bothered that he didn't know who his mother was. Even so, he seemed like a regular guy to us and was always accepted into the group without question.

"Hank was peculiar in several ways. He was a huge fan of horror movies and war movies (yes, kids, we did have TV back then) and he had an exaggerated fear of snakes. On the few occasions when we had the good fortune to kill or catch a snake, the kid having possession always was sure to see that Hank got a close look at it, usually by throwing the creature at him. Hank's reaction was scary. He would become absolutely terrified, running from the scene as fast as his legs would carry him, not stopping until he was safely back in his own home. Of course, we knew nothing about 'phobias', we only knew that Hank's reaction was funny and we loved doing things to each other to get a laugh."

"So, with the group of seven all gathered on this fine Spring morning, we began the adventure we referred to as 'walking the creek'. I was the first to arrive and was soon joined by Weed. While we waited for the others, we lit our first cigarette of the day. Weed had managed to pilfer a couple of Pall Malls from his dad's opened pack which had been carelessly left on the coffee table the night before."

"Now kids, as I've told you before, I don't want you to get the idea that smoking is OK. It's not. But in those days, long before the Surgeon General linked it to cancer, it was accepted as a normal, natural thing to do. It was promoted in movies, on TV and in practically every other ad in major magazines. We thought that the more you smoked, the cooler you were. I have long since quit and I advise you never to start."

"Anyway, about the time we finished our smoke, the Jenkins boys showed up, followed a few minutes later by Pork, accompanied by the ever present SCRAPE …SCRAPE … SCRAPE of 'Old Faithful's chain guard."

"'Hey boys!" he yelled. ""Ya'll ready to catch some fish ? I brought along my baitcaster today. While ya'll stand on the bank with your scrawny ole cane poles, I'm gonna git out there where the big 'uns live.'" He sure thought that bait caster was something special."

"'Oh, sure thing, Pork,'" Weed allowed. "'You'll spend most of the day pickin' out bird nests, like always.'"

"'Oh, we'll see about that. I've been practicin' every day and I've done got pretty good with this thing!'" Pork retorted."

"Larry and Leroy were anxious to get started but the Larsen twins weren't yet here so they suggested we kill some time throwing to the line."

"What's 'throwing to the line', Gramps, Ellie asked.

"Oh, it's just a little game we played with our spare change, which, believe me, wasn't much in those days. The way it works is that you draw a line in the dirt and step off about ten paces. Then each kid would toss a coin toward the line and the one closest to the line won the other's money."

"Larry, the older brother was the best in our group at this game and nearly always ended up winning. Being from the poorest family, we all figured he worked harder at it than the rest of us and needed the money more. Why, on a good day, he might win a dollar or even a dollar and a half! Of course, there were times when each of us might get hot and win, but Larry was the most consistent."

"Lucky for the rest of us, Tom and Tim showed up before Larry got all our money and we hid our bikes in brush alongside the creek and began our journey. There was no real hurry as we all knew that, however far we walked, we had to walk the same distance back to retrieve our bikes."

"There were several large pools along the two to three

mile course we usually walked and it was at these sites that we usually stopped to fish or swim or to just lie in the sun."

"On this particular day I had been granted the privilege of bringing my father's old .410 single shot shotgun. Having only three shells, I did not waste any of them needlessly. On this day, though, I got the opportunity to actually fire the gun. It's still a wonder to me that no one was injured."

"It happened like this: We had stopped for a smoke break at the first big pool which was probably only about twenty feet wide and maybe three to four feet deep. Tom and Tim along with Leroy and Larry had immediately stripped and waded into the cool clean waters, laughing and splashing each other as they advanced."

"Suddenly, Hank, who had been lounging on a big rock enjoying a smoke, yelled, "'SNAKE, SNAKE!! GET OUTTA THE WATER!!. THERE'S A SNAKE IN THERE!!'"

"At exactly that same moment, there was a huge splash as a thick water moccasin hit the water, having fallen from an overhanging limb. This was accompanied by so much yelling and splashing that it was hard to separate one body from another. In the midst of it all, the snake was coolly swimming along, making his escape. He probably had no intention of harming anyone but I was not about to relay on his good intentions. Besides I had not brought along the .410 for no reason. I immediately threw the gun to my shoulder and cut loose with a shot at the snake which was now in the middle of the four thrashing bodies."

"The loud 'BOOM' was followed by sheer pandemonium. All four boys hit the water simultaneously and submerged themselves for as long as they could hold their breaths.

An immediate panic overwhelmed me as I did not know if any of them had been hit. I could just imagine having to explain to a parent how I had managed to kill their son. The second worry was that I could not see the snake so I didn't know his whereabouts. I feared the worst as I waited for the guys to emerge from the water. A huge 'Thank you God' sprang from my lips as they all surfaced with no apparent injuries, other than a knot on Leroy's head from hitting a small rock on the bottom."

"'Skid, you idiot! You almost shot us,' Larry yelled as he waded in my direction."

"'Aw, c'mon, Larry, I missed you by at least a foot'" I admitted. "'But I was afraid the snake was gonna bite you. I had to do somethin'.'"

"'Well, you coulda' waited for us to get clear, couldn't you?'"

"'Yeah, I guess,'" I said. "'I just didn't have time to think.'"

"'Well, next time, how 'bout a little warning, OK?'" He was beginning to calm down, for which I was grateful."

"I promise, next time I will,'" I said. I was extremely relieved that no one had gotten hurt, but could not suppress a smile at the spectacle I'd just witnessed. Soon the gang had dried off and dressed before resuming their trek down the creek, spirits not dampened in the least by the close brush they'd just had with death. In their minds they were indestructible, immortal and could overcome anything they might encounter."

"That's just the way we thought back then, kids. We were "bullet-proof" and would live forever. We had many other adventures walkin' the creek but that's about all the time we have for today. We better get on back to the house in time for supper or your Gramma's sure to be peeved."

"OK, Gramps" they chimed together, as they began gathering their things for the long walk back to the house. It had been a good day and they were sure the meal Gramma had waiting for them would top it off perfectly. In that, they were not disappointed.

About the Author

Born in Macon, GA in 1949, Stephen Davis attended Lanier High School, graduating in 1967. He continued his education at the University of Georgia, earning a BBA degree in Business Administration (1971). In extra-curricular activities, he earned three varsity letters at Lanier and four at UGA, all as a member of the small-bore rifle team. As an ROTC cadet at UGA, he was immediately commissioned a 2nd Lt in the US Army following graduation and served a 2-year active duty stint at Ft. Benning, GA. Following his active duty status in 1973, he embarked upon a 47-year civilian career as a Georgia Banker, retiring in December, 2019. He enjoys reading, fishing and golf. He married Sandra Baker Walden in 1990. They have raised five children, all now adults and have been blessed with six grandchildren. They currently reside in Lizella, GA and are active in their local church.

Made in the USA
Coppell, TX
30 October 2025

62108046R10105